LONG TIME PASSING

OTHER BOOKS BY LINDA CREW

LONG TIME PASSING

LINDA CREW

DELACORTE PRESS

Published by
Delacorte Press
Bantam Doubleday Dell Publishing Group, Inc.
1540 Broadway
New York, New York 10036

Library of Congress Cataloging-in-Publication Data
Crew, Linda.
    Long time passing / Linda Crew.
        p.   cm.
    Summary: In her sophomore year of high school Kathy Shay begins
the process of coming of age in a small town in Oregon during the
turbulent 1960s.
    ISBN 0-385-32496-0
    [1. Interpersonal relations—Fiction. 2. Friendship—Fiction.
3. High schools—Fiction. 4. Schools—Fiction.] I. Title.
PZ7.C86815Lo   1997
[Fic]—dc21   96-54715
                                                      CIP
                                                       AC

The text of this book is set in 11.75-point Minion.
Book design by Julie E. Baker

Manufactured in the United States of America
October 1997
10 9 8 7 6 5 4 3 2 1
BVG

For Theresa Nelson

A faithful friend is the medicine of life.
—ECCLESIASTICUS 6:16

CHAPTER
1

SHE'D BE A winner.

Or a loser.

In.

Or out.

The vice principal would either call her name.

Or not.

Whose idea was this, anyway? Which sadistic mind plotted this spectacle as the finale of the year's first pep rally?

Kathy Shay took a deep breath of the stuffy auditorium air. Look at me, she thought. I'm a wreck. Even the agonizing wait to actually perform her rally tryout routine yesterday hadn't been *this* bad.

Ooops—doing it again. Weren't times like these bad enough without this infernal compulsion to stand back and watch herself suffering through them?

Now the coaches were introducing the members of the J.V. football team—as if everyone didn't already know perfectly well who'd made it and who hadn't.

Her friend Diane tilted toward her. "Did you watch that new show last night?"

"What?"

"*Star Trek*. It's so cool."

Oh, why didn't they hurry up with the rally squad announcements?

"It's science fiction," Diane went on. "In the first episode last week—"

As Diane whispered and the coach called the names of the football team members, Kathy scanned the auditorium. Did the other fourteen sophomore candidates feel as awful as she did? Probably. Who wasn't desperate to be a winner? Who didn't long to walk the halls of Chintimini High as a standout, no longer anonymous in the huge class of six hundred?

She shifted in her hard wooden seat, wondering how she'd react if she made the squad. Maybe a small, involuntary bounce, hands to her cheeks in thrilled disbelief, a settling back as others reached over to congratulate her?

"Gary Fry," the coach called.

Kathy snapped to attention. She watched her old boyfriend take the stage, then traded looks with Diane—hers suffering, Diane's sympathetic. Would she ever stop going sick at the sight of him? She sighed. Her only hope was winning a spot on the rally squad. That might help get him back.

But what if she didn't make it? With the winners being decided by a vote of the student body, the losers might just as well wear buttons—NOT POPULAR.

Now her twin brother, Kenny, was climbing the stage steps to cheers. As he turned and faced out, his eyes, sweeping the audience, met hers for just a second—about as close as she and her brother ever came to acknowledging each other in public. Lots of people didn't realize they were related, let alone twins.

Finally the entire team was in place, each member with his feet spread, hands clasped at the small of his back, face radiating pleased pride. When they'd been thoroughly applauded, they took their seats, and the vice principal came to the podium.

"Now," he said, "the moment you've been waiting for—the five girls chosen by the sophomore class as its junior varsity rally squad."

The auditorium buzzed, then hushed.

Kathy focused on the gold letters stitched to the upper corner of the stage's blue velvet curtain—CLASS OF 1966, a gift from last year's graduating seniors.

"Debbie Andrews."

Squeals. Cheers.

"Kathy—"

She started to push up—

"Walters."

Sank back, cheeks burning, heart racing. Close call. Chintimini High had a million Kathys.

Each name called lowered her chances.

And then it was over.

Five names.

Not hers.

She hadn't made it.

A numbness came over her.

"What a rip-off," Diane said.

Girls nearby stole peeks at Kathy. Such a particular horror—people knowing you wanted something, people watching you not get it.

She became aware of the hubbub of hugging in the section of the auditorium where the Chosen Ones

3

were sitting together. And *had* been since the assembly began, come to think of it.

"Tell me this wasn't rigged," Diane said. "Every one of them went to Jefferson Elementary."

"Well, it *was* a vote," Kathy murmured.

"Still."

The Chosen Ones gathered onstage, blushing and weeping. Five bouffant hairdos, five pleated skirts. Kathy saw that even with her longer hair flipped up on the ends, parted on the side, and clipped with a barrette, she wouldn't have fit in.

Mercifully, the assembly ended. As the throng of students swept Kathy up the auditorium aisle, she forgot about people watching her. She was too busy watching herself. How exactly do I feel? she kept wondering.

And then she recognized it stealing over her, faint but unmistakable, a completely unexpected sense of . . . could it be? Yes: *relief.* Not at losing—hey, no one wanted to be a loser. But relief just the same. Because things had suddenly become so clear. She was standing at a fork in the road, she saw now.

She stopped just outside the front doors, blinking in the hazy autumn sunshine. Setting her books at her feet, she unfastened her barrette, ran a new center part through her hair, and shook it out. Then she scooped up her books and started down the sweep of curved steps, taking them slowly, deliberately, as her classmates streamed by on either side.

After all, this was *her* story, wasn't it? And she was the main character? Well, it sure wasn't going to be the story of her defeat. This was going to be the story of how she came to her senses in a flash of insight. And okay, it's true she was playing this scene in a flippy pleated skirt just like those of the Chosen Ones,

4

but not for long. Because hadn't she always known deep down she wasn't the cheery, rah-rah type? The vote of the student body had simply delivered confirmation of this like a long overdue wake-up slap.

And who cared about Gary? Or any other boyfriend, for that matter? She was sick of all the junior high going-steady stuff, the pairing up that was more a group process of note passing and gossip than a relationship between two people. And what had Gary ever done but keep her from being her real self with his snide remarks about Joan Baez and Peter, Paul and Mary and his know-it-all attitude about everything from the best hairdos for girls to the U.S. policy in Vietnam.

Starting now, she thought, climbing onto the yellow school bus, she would go her own way.

CHAPTER
2

"SO?" HER MOTHER asked, meeting her at the front door in wincing anticipation. "Did you make it?"

"Nope."

"Oh, honey . . ."

"It's okay, Mom."

"But you worked so hard on that routine."

"I'm glad, though. Really. This was meant to be."

"Well, there's still drill team . . ."

"No, Mom, you don't get it. I'm already wondering why on earth I tried out in the first place. This is something that's been coming on for a long time. It's just, like, the final nail in the coffin of my future as a cheerleader."

"Oh."

"That's not going to freak you out, is it?" Her mother had been Yell Queen or something back in high school and obviously considered rally a worthwhile goal.

"Freak me out? Where do you get these expressions? No, it's your life, honey. You know I just want you to be happy."

"Good." Kathy marched into her room and shoved

open the sliding closet door—*Bang*. Peter Pan–collar blouses, plaid skirts. She pawed through them. Not one single thing that would look decent on the cover of a folk music record album. Where had all these stupid clothes come from?

Well, she and her mother had made them, of course, but the question was, why? What could she have been thinking? She needed dresses you could wear running across a meadow, made from fabric that looked like you'd woven it on your own loom.

She started pulling clothes off hangers and throwing them on her bed.

"What are you doing?" Her mother stood in the doorway.

"Sorting my clothes. These can go to Goodwill."

Her mother's eyebrows went up. "This looks like a full-scale dumping."

"Well, these just aren't *me* anymore."

"All because you didn't make rally?"

"No, not just because of that. That's just a sign. I don't know how I thought I could be a folksinger and a rally squad type at the same time, anyway."

Her mother regarded the nearly empty closet. "But what are you going to wear? We can't afford to go out and buy a whole new wardrobe."

"I don't want one. I want to get away from all this . . . this materialism."

"Materialism?"

"Yes! You know—excessive, conspicuous consumption."

"Oh."

"Anyway, I've got some baby-sitting money. Enough to make a couple of dresses. I've definitely got to have something for the hootenanny."

7

"I suppose." Her mother ran her hand over a jumper she'd made, now in the discard pile. "I could take you down now to pick out patterns and fabric, if you want. I'll have to be back to start dinner . . ."

"No! I mean, thanks, but . . . I can do it myself." Looking at each item of cast-off clothing, Kathy remembered its purchase or creation. And suddenly it was so clear: Her mother was behind every single article. To shop with her was to be steered and persuaded, to be lectured on quality of fabric and a pattern's flattering lines so that in the end, Kathy's clothes all screamed the same message: *My mother approves of me!*

Same story with this new house they'd moved into only a few weeks before. For years her mother had wanted out of their grid-block subdivision. She'd always dreamed of living up among the trees in a hilly neighborhood of winding streets.

As the house on Firwood was being built, she'd talked to Kathy about her room, what fun it would be to plan and decorate it. Kathy lost interest as soon as she realized there was absolutely no chance of having a Greenwich Village coffeehouse brick wall in this bedroom, and all *help plan* actually meant was being allowed to choose between sand beige and ivory for the wall paint.

"So what exactly is this hootenanny thing?" her mother asked.

"People just get up and sing."

"And you want to do that? You're not nervous?"

"Can't be any worse than making a fool of myself at rally tryouts. And Mom? There's one other thing. I'd really like to get my ears pierced before then."

"Oh, Kathy, don't start this."

"What? Lots of people are doing it."

"You know how I feel about pierced ears. It looks . . . cheap."

"Oh, come on."

"I'm sorry, Kathy, but it's hard for me to get away from the ideas *I* grew up with. Women who pierced their ears were . . . well, not nice."

Kathy rolled her eyes.

"And I always remember this woman I saw at a carnival. Her earlobes stretched way down. The hole was an inch long." Her nose wrinkled. "You wouldn't want that."

"My earlobes are not going to stretch from wearing teeny little rings."

"I know they're not, because you're not going to get your ears pierced."

"Mom! It's my life and you just want me to be happy, remember?"

Silently her mother began folding the unwanted clothes.

"So what if I just went and did it?" Kathy said.

"Well, then . . . then you'd better forget college money from us!"

"You're kidding."

"No, I'm not."

"Wouldn't you hate having to explain to people someday that I didn't get a decent education because I pierced my ears? After all, remember the big nylons battle."

"Don't remind me!"

Kathy had suffered all through the cold and rainy winter of seventh grade because her mother refused to let her wear nylons, and Kathy insisted on making do with those wretched footies rather than humiliate

9

herself with ankle socks. "It's ridiculous!" Mom kept saying. "When I was your age I was wearing saddle shoes and bobby socks." As if this had been some well-thought-out and practical decision on her part, and not just as much a nod to conformity as Kathy's yearning for nylons.

"I may have been wrong," her mother said now. "Believe it or not, I didn't enjoy watching you go around bare-legged as a plucked chicken. But clothes are just temporary. Piercing your ears is permanent."

"Oh, Mom—"

"And pierced ears is where I'm drawing the line!"

CHAPTER
3

"EVER THINK ABOUT hopping a freight train?" Kathy said to Diane, who was working alongside her in the art room.

"No, you?"

"Not really. Sometimes I wonder if that's even for real. I mean, maybe train hopping is just something they put in Peter, Paul and Mary songs."

"Maybe," Diane said. She obviously did not consider this worthy of a whole lot of thought.

"Probably a plain old passenger train would be fine," Kathy said. "Actually, I'd settle for just saying goodbye to someone at the station."

Diane glanced at Kathy's pastel. "Is that what this is? Because I'm not sure passenger trains have cabooses."

"Oh."

Kathy's composition showed a brown-haired girl (herself) standing on a railway platform with her guitar, watching a train pull away. Dulling down the colors with gray had been a satisfying experiment— made the scene look moodier, depressing, more like a gloomy day here in Oregon. She'd fussed and struggled over the toes of the girl's boots, though, which persisted in turning up at an improbable angle.

"So who are you wishing would leave, anyway?" Diane said.

"Nobody. Besides, it's not the getting rid of somebody. It's how poignant it would be if someone you loved had to leave."

"What's *poignant* mean?"

"Oh, sort of painful."

"You're hoping for painful stuff?"

"But it's beautiful too, see?"

Diane gave her a straight look, then crossed her eyes, her favorite comment on anything that struck her as particularly nutty. She flipped back her hair.

"Hey," Kathy said. "When did you get your ears pierced? Your mother let you?"

Diane shrugged. "Didn't ask her."

"Huh. And she's not taking away your college money?"

"*What?*"

"Never mind." Kathy had always thought she and Diane were alike, even down to the way they dealt with their mothers. But maybe not. "So, did it hurt?"

"A little." Diane's sleek dark flip swung forward as she bent back over her work. She was bringing to life another horse in motion.

"You're so good at those," Kathy said.

Diane cast a critical eye at her sketch. She'd been drawing horses, she said, since she picked up her first crayon. By the time she and Kathy met in junior high, she was already proficient.

Kathy had never been horse crazy like so many girls. In theory, though, she adored them. Fair maids in old ballads were always leaping on horses to ride off and save their true loves. *Go bridle me my milk white steed . . . Go bridle me my pony . . . I will ride to London's court . . . to plead for the life of Geordie.* That would be cool—galloping across wildflower meadows with all your yards of hair billowing out behind you . . .

She focused again on her own drawing. Trains were probably a more realistic daydream than golden-maned horses. Or were they? She heard train whistles at night, watched at crossings while flatcars laden with lumber clanked past. But what about passenger trains? Nobody around here ever seemed to be going anywhere on a train.

"Diane, do we even have a train station in Chintimini?"

"Albany's the closest. Why?"

"I don't know," she said dreamily, going back to work.

She loved the smell of the art room—oil paints, chalk pastels, the earthy scent of wet clay drifting in from the adjacent pottery room. She loved it the same way she loved walking through her father's art supply store—all those materials just waiting to be combined into something . . .

"Hey," Diane said, "are we going to the football game tonight?"

"Well, I'm not. Didn't I tell you? I'm singing at the hootenanny."

"Oh. Who you going with?"

"Nobody."

"All by yourself?"

"Well, you'd rather go to the game, right?"

"You won't be mad at me?"

"Diane! No. You should do what you want to do."

"Okay. Geez, Kath, you amaze me."

"What?"

"Where do you get the nerve to just get up and do these things in front of people?"

AS KATHY STOOD in the cafeteria doorway that night, her stomach fluttered with the feeling that maybe, just maybe, her life was about to begin.

Where had all these interesting-looking people come from? The other side of town? Everyone, it seemed, was just letting their hair grow. Not a crew cut, not a bubble cut in sight. She was supremely glad at that moment she'd had the foresight to be the first girl at her junior high to grow out her bangs.

Her new beige smock dress fit in okay too. It had been worth the hassle with her mother. "This is a *maternity* pattern," Mom kept saying. "With your nice flat tummy, I can't imagine why you'd want to wear this." And when the dress was made, its plainness was the cause of great concern. "It needs something. Beads, or maybe a scarf?" Close call, but Kathy finally escaped without any of what her mother referred to as accessories.

She signed the performer registry and picked her way to a spot by the arched brace of the cafeteria roof. Settling down on the linoleum, she unlatched the case and took out her guitar, her prize possession. Nearby heads turned.

"Framus?" a boy asked.

She nodded.

"Nice."

Yes, it was. A year of baby-sitting money, and worth every nickel. She fiddled with the tuning, mostly for something to look busy about, since she'd tuned it and practiced her song—"Maid of Constant Sorrow"—several times right before she came.

Looking around, she began studying details of dress, picking up on the grown-up smell of cigarette smoke in hair and clothing, catching snatches of conversation that made her feel as if everyone except her knew each other.

Then she spotted the girl with the amazing hair. It flowed down her back all the way to her waist. Here was a person, clearly, who had anticipated the future coolness of long hair way before anyone else.

Why didn't I think of that? Kathy chided herself. Why did I stick so long with that stupid puffy bubble cut? That ridiculous little velvet bow clipped at the top of my bangs? Just because Gary Fry once said this style looked "bitchin' " ...

Oh, sometimes she couldn't help wishing she'd been born full-grown only about two weeks ago—then she wouldn't have to keep remembering all the dumb things she'd done when she was young.

Clearly this long-haired girl had no embarrassing past to haunt her. Her dress was drapey black velvet. Pierced ears, of course. One hammered silver earring. And Samson sandals, leather thongs laced all the way up her calves. Kathy had always wanted a pair. And more, she longed for the nerve it would take to wear them. Because people were bound to stare.

Finally, a boy with Coke-bottle glasses tapped the mike and said he would start things off with the antiwar anthem they all knew and could join in on—"Where Have All the Flowers Gone?"

15

This is it, Kathy thought, adding her voice to the others. These are the people I've been looking for.

"Where have all the young girls gone? Long time passing . . ."

SIX PERFORMERS AND six folk songs later, the long-haired girl stepped up on the small platform stage with her guitar. God, she was so beautiful. Yes, I've suffered, her look said. I've seen a thing or two. And those huge, soulful eyes. Surely Bob Dylan had someone just like her in mind, Kathy thought, when he came up with "Sad-eyed Lady of the Lowland." The girl lifted her face into the spotlight, closed her eyes, and in a high soprano began to sing.

"I am a maid . . . of constant sor . . . row . . ."

Oh, no! Kathy sat, stunned, for a full minute before starting to rack her brains for another number. "Fair and Tender Maidens"? No, she'd overheard another girl saying she was doing that. "The Water Is Wide"? She hadn't practiced that for ages . . . Okay, "Wildwood Flower." But what were the words?

Then her eyes fell on a dark-haired boy sitting near the stage. His cheeks were flushed red. His hair was more than dark: It was black. Hey, that's it!

"Kathy Shay."

She picked her way through the sprawled-out crowd and into the light, slipping the embroidered guitar strap over her shoulder.

> *"Black, black, black is the color*
> *Of my true love's hair*
> *His lips are something wondrous fair*

The purest eyes and the bravest hands
I love the ground whereon he stands . . ."

Her low, mellow voice sounded good with the mike, she thought, echoing around the cavernous cafeteria. She'd been scared, starting, but now it was just her and the guitar in the pool of light and she could have happily gone on and on.

"If he on earth, no more I see
My life will surely fade away . . ."

The applause sounded so good as she stepped off the stage. Felt so warm. She'd done it.

The black-haired boy got up, announcing a song he'd written himself. With a driving, insistent strum he launched into something sounding suspiciously like Dylan's "Masters of War," right down to the growl he used to deliver it.

"We'll never obey your commandments of war . . ."

Suddenly lights blazed on. A microphone squealed.

"Okay, the party's over."

A rumble of protest rolled through the crowd. Kathy blinked against the brightness.

It was the vice principal at the mike. "I think you're all aware that James Holderread had been forbidden to participate tonight. The rules have been violated. The hootenanny's over."

"We hardly got started!" someone hollered, and the crowd roared agreement. "Let him sing!"

"Everyone will please leave now."

A sullen, mumbling mass rose unevenly and shuffled toward the doors.

Bewildered, Kathy packed up her guitar. Moving out with the crowd, she glanced around for an explanation.

"Why's he forbidden?" she asked the closest, least intimidating-looking girl.

"Probably that locker protest thing. Hey, you were good."

"Oh, thanks. Um, what protest?"

"About the searches? He got a bunch of people to sit in the halls—"

"He's not really just a sophomore, is he?" someone interrupted.

"That's right."

"Geez. Doesn't waste any time stirring things up, does he?"

"The narcs had to drag people away," the girl said, "to get at the lockers."

"Narcs?" Kathy asked.

"Yeah, narcotics officers? Looking for drugs?"

"Oh."

"Well, actually, it was probably just the vice principal and a couple of P.E. teachers, but what's the diff?"

The chill autumn air outside was a shock after the warmth of the cafeteria. Kathy stood undecidedly, watching people leaving in pairs and groups. She hadn't minded coming alone; leaving alone was something else.

Life, it seemed, hadn't quite started after all.

Clutching the pay phone, waiting for her parents to answer, she saw the sad-eyed girl surrounded by her friends.

After the sixth ring, Kathy became aware of the roar from the football field and remembered—her parents would be at the game. She'd have to go around to the field to find them. She replaced the receiver, picked up her guitar case, and started walking.

In the distance, she could hear the guy who'd brought the gathering to such an abrupt end. He was shouting the lines of his hopelessly derivative song into the darkness.

CHAPTER
4

"DID YOU HEAR the drama department's doing *The Miracle Worker*?" Diane said at their locker the next Friday.

"Really?" Kathy said. "That was an amazing movie."

"Yeah. My mom thinks I should try out because Helen Keller is supposed to be six years old, so they'll need somebody short. I'm only five feet."

"Don't you have to be in drama club or something?"

"No, tryouts are open. They start Monday after school."

"Well, hey," Kathy said. "I'm only five-one."

"Good. *You* try out then."

"Maybe I will."

SHE PHONED DIANE several times over the weekend. "Just come with me," she pleaded when Diane said she didn't want to audition. "I can't walk in there by myself."

"Gimme a break! You tried out for rally when I was

too chicken to do it with you. You went to the hootenanny by yourself."

"Well, see, that just shows you."

"Huh?"

"Shows how scared I am. Because you know it's not
like me to be chicken about something like this. So,
please?"

THANK GOD DIANE had given in, Kathy thought as
she pulled open the heavy auditorium door for the
two of them Monday afternoon.

"See that girl?" Diane whispered as they took seats
halfway down the aisle. "The one with black tights?"

"Which?" Kathy looked toward a group standing
around the front rows. "They're all wearing black
tights."

"The blonde. That's Val Bodine. People are saying
for sure she's going to be Helen."

"Thanks, Diane."

"I'm just telling you what I heard. She's a senior
and I guess she's been in lots of stuff before."

Another of the girls was someone Kathy had
noticed in the halls. How could you miss her? Six feet
tall and incredibly thin. Her hair frizzed out of control, with a strange streak of gray flaring from her
center part.

Just as Mr. Corwin, the director, came to the front
with his clipboard, the back auditorium door opened.
Heads turned.

The girl from the hootenanny, the sad-eyed one. As
the girl passed, Kathy caught a whiff of violet cologne
laced with cigarette smoke. The girl's incredible hair
lifted behind her as she went striding down the aisle.

21

The hootenanny guy with the Coke-bottle glasses waved her to a seat he'd saved.

Mr. Corwin made some remark and the black tights bunch laughed—an in-joke. Great. Was this going to be just like rally? The group already sitting together would automatically get all the good parts?

Mr. Corwin was pleased, he said, with the unusually big turnout. He hoped people weren't feeling too nervous.

The jittery laughter made Kathy realize: Even the drama kids were scared.

A couple of them passed out information sheets.

Bummer, Kathy thought, having to write *none* under experience. And the blank for the part you hoped to play? Seemed so presumptuous to put *Helen.* Sure—no experience whatsoever and you're hoping for the lead.

"What's the matter?" Diane said, noticing Kathy's pen poised.

"Nothing. Just thinking." Where had she got the idea that it wasn't quite . . . *nice,* somehow, to aim for the top, to admit you wanted to win. You weren't supposed to be competitive. Maybe boys could. But girls weren't supposed to be . . . aggressive.

Who decided this, anyway? Kathy frowned and in bold letters printed *HELEN.*

As the students were called up to read, Kathy tried to catch their names. The beanpole girl was Winnie somebody. The boy with the thick glasses was David. And the sad-eyed girl was Julia McCullough, already reading the part of Helen's teacher, Annie Sullivan, with a convincing Irish accent.

After the first round of readings, Mr. Corwin asked all the potential Helens to come up onstage. Kathy and Diane made big eyes at each other and pushed up from their seats.

Mr. Corwin had somebody put a stool and a rag doll in the middle of the stage and told the girls to come across one at a time, pretending to be blind.

The difficulty for most of them, Kathy saw, waiting her turn in the wings, was in forgetting themselves. Several seemed ready to giggle. One or two, proud of their own prettiness, simply couldn't abandon themselves to the sort of out-of-control flailing Kathy remembered from the movie.

Val was good, though. You could tell she'd been practicing. Diane wasn't bad either.

Finally, Kathy's turn. She whirled around the stage, arms flung wide, palms seeking, and managed to stumble into the stool without seeming to anticipate it. A murmur from the audience told her this had been effective.

When the group broke to leave, Diane leaned into Kathy as they walked up the aisle. "Don't look now, but Val Bodine just shot you one of those classic dagger looks."

"Really?" Kathy brightened, turning.

"I said don't look!" Then Diane lowered her voice another notch. "I think she was saying something about you to that tall one."

"Yeah?"

"Uh-huh. And unless I'm way off base, *you*, my friend, are being regarded as a threat."

ON WEDNESDAY A callback list was posted with Kathy, Val, Diane, and two other girls down for the part of Helen. Then, after another intense afternoon of readings and blind tug-of-wars over the rag doll, Mr. Corwin announced he still wasn't ready to do the final casting.

"Please check the callback list again tomorrow morning."

A collective groan. How much more of this could they stand?

BY FRIDAY, THE possibilities for Helen had been narrowed to Val, Diane, and Kathy.

"I think I can safely say," Mr. Corwin told the group, "that these have been, by far, the most exciting and exhausting tryouts we've ever had. I have some very tough choices to make."

Choose me, Kathy prayed, trying to beam this into his brain. Please! I can do it. You won't be sorry!

"I MIGHT ACTUALLY get it!" Kathy told her family at dinner Friday night. "I can't believe it. Ten days ago I wouldn't have dreamed I could be right on the verge of getting a lead part in a play! And it's going to be like a major production."

"Well, it's exciting, honey," Mom said. "But don't get your hopes up."

"That's right," Dad said, "don't count your chickens before they hatch."

Kathy and Kenny traded a look and Kenny mouthed the number forty-two. Their little game— keeping count. *Dad's All-Occasion Clichés.*

"Kenny, is that all you're going to eat?" Mom asked.

Kenny stood up from the table, taking his plate. "You know how it is before a game."

"So Dad's driving you?" Mom asked.

Dad looked up like this was a surprise to him, then nodded quickly, as if to catch up.

"Maybe you should hope Kathy doesn't get in the play, Mom," Kenny said. "You don't want her hanging out with those drama types."

"Oh, Kenny," Kathy said.

"I'll worry about that when we're sure there's something to worry about."

"Right," Dad said. "We'll cross that bridge when we come to it."

Kenny caught Kathy's eye. Forty-three.

After Dad and Kenny were gone, Kathy turned again to her mother. "So you don't think there's even a chance I might get it?"

"I didn't say that," Mom said. "It sounds like you might."

Kathy perked up. "You think so?"

"Kathy! How should I know? I'm only going by what you're telling me. I just don't want to see you disappointed if you don't."

"Well, it's too late. If I don't get this, I *will* be disappointed. Extremely. But listen, Mom. Today he had us do that final scene, the breakthrough moment when Helen remembers *water* is *wa wa* and makes the connection that words stand for things? And guess what? Afterward, I heard people saying that when Julia McCullough and I did it, everyone was crying. Isn't that amazing? Just the best feeling, that we could . . . you know, move people like that. Oh, really, this show is going to be so good . . ."

"Honey, calm down."

"I can't."

Mom sighed. "Well, when will you find out?"

"He's going to post the cast list tomorrow morning."

"On a Saturday?"

"He said the school will be open for sports stuff and he didn't want to keep people in suspense all weekend. Thank goodness! I don't know how I can stand the suspense for one night!"

She hardly slept. Her mind refused to turn off. She kept recalling all the other win-lose situations of her life.

Losing out on rally squad had been public and humiliating, but only briefly. Now she was not so much embarrassed by not getting it as she was by having wanted it in the first place.

Missing out on the Outstanding Music Student award in junior high after everyone told her she was a shoo-in had been a definite bummer, but in the end it was just a certificate. What difference would it have made in her life? None.

And as for winning? The thirty-five-dollar first prize in the Humane Society poster contest had been nice, sure.

But *The Miracle Worker*—these tryouts struck her as a win-lose situation different from anything she'd ever been up against. The prize here—getting in— was better than a certificate or money. With the lead, you'd be cool by definition. It might actually alter the course of your life.

IN THE MORNING, buzzy from lack of sleep, Kathy biked down to the school. The air was chilly and acrid with the smell of rain on burnt fields. As she pedaled, she tried to brace herself. Everyone had said right from the start the part was Val's. People swore Mr. Corwin gave preference to the older kids every time. Still . . .

It has to be me. It just has to be . . .

She pushed her bike across the patio on shaking legs and locked it to the rack.

Inside, to the left down the hall, she saw people at the bulletin board. She beelined toward the list as others eased back.

On the left side were typed the character names. Her eyes ran down to HELEN and followed the dots across.

HELEN . . . she blinked . . . DIANE STEWART.

IT WAS PROBABLY the shock that made it possible for her to get home before she started crying.

"Diane didn't even want to try out!" she wailed to her mother. "She wouldn't have if I hadn't begged her."

Like it mattered now.

"Well," Mom said, "there'll be other plays."

"Not like this!" Kathy pulled her pillow over her head.

From out in the hall Kenny said, "What's going on?" He'd just gotten up and sounded half asleep.

"She didn't get the part," Mom whispered, as if announcing bad news loudly might make it worse.

"I didn't get the part!" Kathy yelled.

"Come on now," Dad said. He was standing in his usual hanging back position in her doorway. "It's not the end of the world."

"Norm," Mom said, "she's upset. Just . . . let her cry."

"I'm only trying to point out," Dad said, "that life does go on. And didn't you say she got a part?"

"Dad, the blind girls are onstage about three minutes."

"Well then, make those the best three minutes of the whole play! Remember, anything worth doing at all is worth doing well."

She cried and cried. The cold she'd been fighting all week flattened her like a steamroller, silenced her with laryngitis. At least this made it easier to beg off talking too long when Diane phoned. What on earth could Kathy say in response to Diane's guilt-tinged amazement? Kathy lay there all weekend, vowing she'd never try for anything again the rest of her life.

She put her hi-fi on the floor so that without getting out of bed, she could dangle her arm over the side and keep dropping the needle on "The Sounds of Silence."

Monday morning, she still felt bad enough to stay home.

"A day off wouldn't hurt you a bit," Mom said. "But how about a day off from Simon and Garfunkel too?"

Kathy dozed awhile. Another day of Mom bringing chicken soup and cinnamon toast on a tray wouldn't be bad.

She woke to find her mother standing in the doorway again, this time dressed up.

"Where you going?"

"Well, to work."

"You're not going to be here?"

"Kathy, I can't call in sick because my fifteen-year-old has the sniffles."

Kathy glanced away, ashamed. She'd actually forgotten, for the moment, her mother's new job at the university health service. And here the whole point of Mom going back to work was to earn money for their college fund.

"So when *do* you come home?"

"Three. Like always."

Like always. Kathy had never stopped to realize her mother planned her day to be there when she and Kenny finished school.

Kathy threw back the covers. "Might as well get up." She headed for the bathroom. "Life does go on, you know."

After all, just because something is a cliché doesn't mean it isn't true.

CHAPTER
5

"YOU MIGHT NOT go with him?" Diane said when Kathy reported that Gary Fry had invited her to the Homecoming Bonfire. They were standing backstage, waiting through rehearsal of the first *Miracle Worker* scene.

"I just said I'd think about it and tell him tomorrow."

"Kathy, I don't believe you."

"What?"

"Well, when I think how upset you were when he broke up with you. No offense, but it got kind of boring. I mean, that's all you talked about last summer. And Karen Daley's party?"

"Don't remind me."

That awful night would be stuck in her head forever, thanks to Karen's extremely limited record collection. For the rest of her life, Kathy was sure, "The House of the Rising Sun" would trigger a vision of Gary Fry and Mary Becky Whitney, arms wrapped around each other, rocking in place on the Daleys' patio. And her stupid self, standing there against the garage—classic wallflower style—thinking, Well, gee, he's danced with her seventeen times in a row now . . . I'll bet any minute he's going to come over and dance with me.

"Go with him," Diane was urging. "I'll bet he wants to get together again."

"You think so?"

"Duh! Why else would he ask you out?"

Kathy bit her lip. "I guess I am still kind of hung up on him. I don't know, though. I wasn't planning to be a go-team-go type person anymore."

"Hey, this is a date, dummy, not a career plan."

Kathy watched from the wings as Diane went onstage and became Helen Keller. No getting around it. She was amazingly convincing as a blind child— that neat trick she had of rolling one eye back, crossing the other.

"Diane?" Kathy said when she came off. "I've never really told you this before, but . . . I think you're really good."

Diane looked at her. "Thanks, Kath. That means a lot." Then she laughed. "The funny part is, all through that scene, I was thinking about you."

"Me?"

"Yeah, and how you're trying to get out of going to the bonfire with Gary!"

"I'm not trying to get out of it—"

"Hey, call me tonight, okay? I can't talk about this now. Can you believe it? Julia and I have to go do another interview."

"Interview?"

"Yeah, this one's for the real paper. I mean like with an adult reporter. Geez, I bet I can already guess the questions: 'What is the greatest challenge in

31

playing Helen Keller?' " She crossed her eyes in that goofy, isn't-this-nuts way of hers and ran off.

UP IN THE front seat of the Mustang, Gary's older brother was bragging to his date, Homecoming Princess Libby Landforce, about how bitchin' the bonfire was going to be. The Lettermen's Club had been piling up hay bales and wooden pallets for weeks, he said, and for the last few days, they'd guarded it round the clock.

Kathy sat forward. "From what?"

Gary's brother twitched, startled she'd spoken.

"Somebody from Albany might sneak over and torch it," Gary explained. His brother apparently did not deem it fitting that he, personally, should speak to a sophomore girl.

"Why would they do that?" Kathy asked.

Gary's brother snorted, squinting into the rearview mirror with a where'd-you-dig-her-up expression. "To *get* us, of course. After all, we did it to them last month."

"All this over a pile of trash?"

"Kathy," Gary said. "Obviously this is about much more than the bonfire itself, if you can grasp that."

Not exactly the tone you'd expect from a guy hoping to rekindle a romance. But then, so what? Like her mother had said, he didn't have to be the love of her life to be her bonfire date. She ought to be able to just go and have fun. Kathy settled back, studying the smooth, ribbon-encircled ball of honey-colored hair on the top of Libby's head.

"I wish I wasn't even a princess," Libby started telling Gary's brother. "Everyone's going to vote for

Cynthia." She went on analyzing her chances and begging reassurance all the way across town.

How weird to be hearing this, Kathy thought—the raging insecurities of a senior class beauty queen. She concentrated on remembering every word; Diane would enjoy a thorough recounting. Even if this date was a total bust, it was bound to make an interesting story.

"People just don't understand," Libby was saying. "They think, Oh, wow, she's on the court. They have no idea about the pressure."

"Okay, kiddies," Gary's brother said when they reached the parking lot and got out of the car. "Ten. Be here."

The tower of trash was already blazing. Silhouettes of students milling around the flames made the whole thing look like some kind of passionate pagan ritual. Kathy stood in the trampled grass, breathing in the smell of smoke. In urging her to go with Gary, her mother had told her she'd always loved the Homecoming Bonfire so much that even now, if she got a whiff of that smoke, it took her back and made her feel sixteen again.

Kathy turned to Gary, smiling expectantly. Maybe bonfire smoke was magic. Maybe for once everything *would* work out.

Gary stuffed his hands in his jacket pockets and cleared his throat. "I'll get to the point," he said. "Uh, a lot of us think you've gone to the dogs."

Kathy's smile froze. "What?"

"You know what I mean. The people you're hanging around with. The drama types. The hippie peaceniks. Kathy, those are the people who are going to try to get you into drugs."

33

Her mouth fell open.

"Look at you—black tights, baggy beatnik dresses."

"These are jeans, for your information."

"I'm talking about at school. Why can't you just be yourself instead of trying to be Joan Baez or somebody?"

"Hey, what do you care what I wear?" This was unreal. "You really asked me out to tell me this?"

"Even though you might not believe me, I still care about you—as a person, I mean—and I thought it might do you good to go out and do something—you know—normal."

Oh, this was . . . this was . . .

"Get your brother back," she said. "Tell him to take me home."

"Are you kidding? Look, I know you were upset about not making rally, but come on—neither did Mary Becky, and she didn't go nuts."

"You think I give a darn about the stupid rally squad?"

"Kathy, Kathy. Don't be a sore loser."

"I am not a sore loser! I know this is hard for you to believe, but I'm glad I didn't get on it."

"Sure. Geez, you are so touchy. Haven't changed a bit, have you?"

"Actually, I've changed a lot. And one thing—I'm not taking crap from guys like you anymore. I wouldn't even be here except my mother made me."

"Oh, right."

"It's true, so get lost!"

She turned and marched away.

I'll just leave, she thought. I'll walk home. But she couldn't. Some stupid guy would probably grab her and drag her into the bushes and then it would be all her fault for walking alone at night and her parents would be mad at her on top of everything else. Why didn't they lock up the jerky guys and let the girls walk around free, anyway?

She wandered among the clusters of people. This was so unbelievable. Wait till she told Diane. Talk about a story!

Everyone stood in groups or pairs. Was she the only person here alone? She felt so completely alien. But then, she felt that way everywhere lately. Funny that Gary saw her as part of the drama crowd. Anyone knows it takes more than black tights to make you truly part of a group . . .

"Kathy!"

Oh, thank goodness, it was Diane.

"Hey, where's Gary?"

"That jerk," Kathy said. "You won't believe—" She stopped. The boy standing next to Diane—Steve somebody. Hadn't she seen him hanging around with Gary's bunch? "Uh, could I get a ride home with you guys?"

"Well . . ." Diane looked toward the boy.

"Never mind," Kathy said quickly.

Diane gave her an apologetic look, one that promised to pay her back by spilling all the details later.

Kathy left them to each other.

I want to go home, she thought, like Dorothy in Oz. But home wasn't there anymore, was it? Not home as the place where your parents could always make everything all right.

Finally she spotted her brother with his girlfriend, Patty, and a bunch of other kids.

"Hey," she said. "Mom and Dad picking you up?"

"Yeah, why?"

She lowered her voice. "Is there room for me?"

He looked around. He always had a million friends. "We'll stuff you in. What happened to Gary?"

"Tell you later."

He nodded. "The curb out on the corner. Ten?"

"Right." She faded back into the darkness at the edge of the crowd.

It was going to be a long night.

Well, she thought, one thing's sure—twenty years down the line, I won't be getting dreamy-eyed over the smell of bonfire smoke.

CHAPTER
6

"DO YOU EVER wonder," Diane said at lunch one day in January, "if maybe you've already met the guy you're going to marry?"

"Now that," Kathy said, "is a scary thought."

"Why?"

"Well, if I've met him, and it wasn't any big deal, then . . . I don't know, I guess I've just always thought I'd sort of . . . *recognize* the love of my life when he shows up, you know?"

"Like he's going to prance in on a white horse or something?"

"Diane!"

"Better yet, maybe he's wearing a little name sticker that says, 'Hi! I'm So-and-so, Kathy Shay's true love.' "

"Hey, if it turns you on to think you're going to wind up with one of the guys around here, be my guest."

"Um, excuse me?" Diane held up her hand, flashing the ring Steve had given her.

"Okay, I didn't mean him." Kathy usually tried to

forget about Steve. If it wasn't for the good luck of him having the other lunch period, she wouldn't even be able to eat with Diane anymore. "I'm just talking about for me. Personally. I'm still hoping for something more . . . dramatic."

"Dramatic and . . ." Diane shot her a wicked look. "What's that other word of yours? The painful thing? Poignant!"

"Yeah," Kathy said, refusing to back down. "And besides, this would be such a terrible time to fall in love. I couldn't stand it if he got drafted to Vietnam and killed."

"Why do you always imagine the worst?"

"Come on, don't you worry about Steve getting drafted?"

"No."

"Diane—"

"Hey, it's a long time away."

"Steve's a junior."

"Yes. I'm aware of that."

"Well, I don't know," Kathy said, "maybe I'm weird. But things like that just . . . invade my brain. I can't help it." She stuffed her sandwich wrappings in the bag and got up to go.

"Let me guess," Diane said. "The drop?"

"Yup."

On the art teacher's recommendation, Mr. Corwin had asked Kathy to paint the scenic backdrop for the winter play—a fairy-tale production for children.

"But you've been working on that thing every lunch hour this week."

"That's right," Kathy said. "And I'll probably be doing it every day until the play opens."

"What a rip-off, making you do the whole thing."

"No, no, it's not like that. He's *letting* me. I feel . . . honored he's trusting me with it. Besides, it's better if one person does it. You have to keep the style consistent."

Dipping and dabbing, Kathy was happy, working with the purest drive simply to see how her castle in the clouds would turn out. She liked the quiet backstage during lunch hour, the relief from the frenzied cafeteria scene. Here all she had to do was paint and think and remember not to look down when she was balancing at the top of the tallest ladder.

As she shaded the towers of the dream castle, she wondered: Was what Diane said possible? Steve already acted like he owned Diane—it wasn't hard to picture them married. But could Kathy herself have met her future husband? Her mother had once said she figured people married whoever they were going with when they were ready to get married. Not very romantic. What if you met the right person at the wrong time, when you were too young? Or at the right time, you were going with the wrong person? Not that Kathy could buy this business of one true love in all the billions on earth. The odds of never crossing paths would be way too high. But surely somewhere out there she had a soul mate.

ONE DAY AS she returned backstage after mixing a fresh can of paint, she heard voices onstage.

"This is incredible." It sounded like—yes, it was Julia McCullough. "David, can you believe this? I think she's even better than Inge, don't you?"

"No question."

A tingle of pleasure ran up Kathy's spine.

"Looks like you could walk right into the castle, doesn't it?"

"The colors—what a trip."

For some reason, as their voices and footsteps approached, Kathy scurried back across the hall to the shop, heart pounding. She wanted to keep the moment, replay in her mind what they'd said.

The next day in the cafeteria, when Diane had gone off with some new sosh friends, Julia stopped at Kathy's table.

"My dear," she said, "what are you doing here by yourself? Come over to our table."

KATHY SET TO work on the drop for the spring musical with even greater enthusiasm. The *Chintimini Gazette* reviewer had described the castle drop as charming, and charming was nice, but a *Sound of Music* panorama of the Alps—that ought to leave room for true magnificence!

A senior wrote a story for the school newspaper about her. "Artist in the Shadows," he called it, describing her research for the drop, which included a hunt for *National Geographic* photos of the mountains and pictures in the university library of drops from the Broadway production of the show. He managed to make her sound like an intriguing person, the way she haunted the stage in her painting clothes at odd hours. He even compared her efforts to those that had resulted in the ceiling of the Sistine Chapel, a bit of hyperbole Kathy found extremely embarrassing.

Still, it was not unpleasant to walk the halls and have people say, "Oh, sure, you're the artist," or, "Hey, Michelangelo!"

One girl, a junior in Kathy's Algebra II class, even presented her with a smock she'd made in home ec.

"You sewed this for me?" Kathy was overwhelmed at such a kindness from someone whose sole connection to her had been the cheerful daily recognition of their mutual loathing of math.

"Yes, you should have it. Because—you know," she added shyly, "you're the artist."

Kathy began to feel she'd finally found her true calling. When Diane tore the rules for *Seventeen Magazine*'s annual art contest from the March issue and handed them to her, entering seemed the only logical thing to do.

She went home and spread her collected artwork all over her bed and floor.

"What's going on?" her mother said, standing at her door.

"I'm entering this." Kathy snatched the magazine page from her desk and waved it toward her mother. "I'm choosing which things to put in the portfolio I send them."

Her mother took the page. "Five hundred dollars first prize. Wouldn't *that* be something."

"Yeah. I'd be happy with one of the twenty-five-dollar honorable mentions, though—just for the recognition. Hey, Mom." She held up two watercolors. "This or this?"

Mom cocked her head. "Well, I like the still life."

"Do you?" Kathy frowned. "I think I'll send the other."

Mom sighed. Then she said, "You know, honey, they must get thousands of entries."

"Yeah. So?"

"I wouldn't want you to get your hopes up."

41

"Mom. If you never got your hopes up, you'd never try anything. Besides, somebody's got to win. I don't see why it couldn't be me."

"Okay, okay." Mom had gone back to the contest rules. "So there's a short story contest too."

"Uh-huh." Kathy was trying to decide whether to include a certain pen-and-ink drawing or an oil on canvas board. The oil was better, but the board would cost more to mail . . .

"Ever think of entering that?" her mother said.

"Entering what?"

"The writing contest."

"Mom, I'm an artist, not a writer. And look—the story has to be at least two thousand words. That's long! You have to type it too." The typewriter she'd been given at Christmas ("Every girl should learn to type") had been shoved under her desk to gather dust.

"What about that Anne-Frank-in-the-bomb-shelter story you wrote? I thought that was great. And I could do the typing."

"Mom."

"What?"

"Why are you bugging me about this?"

"Am I? Bugging you?"

"Well, what do you call it when you tell me *not* to get my hopes up over the contest I want to enter, but I *should* get my hopes up over the one I *don't* want to enter?"

Mom laughed. "Maybe we think that's our job as mothers? Keep everything evened out? Actually it's probably just that mailing a few sheets of paper would be a lot cheaper and easier than shipping off a portfolio!"

She helped package the artwork between sheets of

cardboard, and when it was ready, Kathy wrote *Seventeen*'s address on the front in bold felt pen.

New York City.

Seemed like everything happened there. Before, she'd imagined singing in some Greenwich Village coffeehouse. Now she had a new reason to go there, a new dream.

She pictured herself walking down a New York City sidewalk carrying an artist's portfolio, looking up at all the skyscrapers . . .

No, scratch that. She wouldn't look up because, hey, she'd been around. By now she's way too sophisticated to gawk like some hick. She'd be striding straight ahead, full of purpose. She'd have an appointment. Art directors would be expecting her up in one of those buildings, eager to see what sorts of wonderful things would come to light when she opened her portfolio . . .

CHAPTER 7

"KATHY?" MOM SAID, looking out the kitchen window. "Are those your friends?"

"What?"

"Some people are . . . sitting in our driveway."

Kathy joined her at the window. Outside, Julia, David, and Val sat with their backs against her parents' Chevy Impala, faces held up to the weak spring sun. Julia was smoking, David had a kazoo in his mouth, Val was wearing a broad-brimmed felt hat with a plume that Kathy recognized from the school's costume closet.

Kathy dashed off to grab her favorite frayed sweater.

"Honestly," Mom said, "why don't they come to the door?"

Kenny took a milk carton from the fridge and swigged. "Because they're weirdos."

"Lay off," Kathy said, embarrassed by her friends, embarrassed by the boring middle-class house in which they'd found her, thrilled they'd come in the first place.

"Is that Val Bodine?" Mom said, putting her hand over her heart. "Oh my God, June must be dying a thousand deaths."

"Who?"

"June Bodine, her mother!"

"You know her mother?" Kathy said, dismayed.

"Of course! She was in Aunt Pat's class."

"See you," Kathy said. Honestly. Couldn't anybody ever be new and mysterious, free of her mother's hometown family histories?

Julia and David and Val rose, wrapping Kathy in elaborate hugs. Then they all jumped into Julia's father's car and took off.

THE MAGIC OF being drawn into their circle— that's what Kathy would remember from the spring of 1967.

Finally she had an official position on that stage known as the cafeteria.

The intellectuals clustered upstage left, the far corner, sincerely uninterested in attracting attention. These were mostly boys, the chess champs, the ones destined to play darts at the Senior All Night Party before they took off for MIT.

The country kids headed upstage right. Quiet kids in Future Farmers jackets, they lived too far out to stay after school for activities, and probably had to go home and milk cows anyway.

The hoods hung out upstage too, but only during the wettest weather; normally they lurked around the trees along the patio curb, smoking.

The jocks and soshes, the loudest, jokiest bunch, dominated front and center. We are the In-crowd.

45

Look how much fun we're having! Don't you wish you were truly one of us, all you who hang around the edges?

Kenny belonged with them, of course, and couldn't understand why Kathy even cared what they were up to. "We're just having fun," he'd say. "Anyway, the drama crowd shows off more than anybody."

No denying this. Kathy's new friends occupied a cluster of tables in the first row by the windows, and favored flamboyant entrances from the hall's double doors, occasionally announcing themselves with tooting kazoos. They were forever running lines from the current show or some scene for drama class, raving in loud foreign accents. Kathy envied their boldness, even though she sometimes wanted to slide under the table when she noticed Gary Fry watching.

Still, to belong was wonderful. To have a place at the table, a ride in Julia's car, the offer of a flower to wear behind her ear like the rest of them. To share in the manic gaiety that seemed some weird antidote to the scenes of televised war that nightly invaded each home.

On Kathy's birthday, Julia presented her with a thrift store pocket watch on a brown velvet ribbon. "The gift of time," she said mysteriously, and Kathy could only nod, enchanted.

She was allowed to join the debates on such topics as exactly how they might know when the coming revolution had actually begun. Or whether it would be worth it to cut one's hair for the privilege of playing the role of Joan of Arc onstage.

Kathy was enthralled by hints of the other people in her friends' lives, cryptic references to forbidden places and incidents. "When the cops showed up that night . . . the last time I hitched to Eugene . . . a man I used to know . . ." (Not a boy, a man!) They threw out the names of musicians faster than you could say "Wait a minute—who?" Kweskin, Rush, Paxton, Ochs, the Holy Modal Rounders . . .

And the mystery of Julia's one silver earring. A friend, she said, was wearing the other. No further explanation. Just "a friend."

You'd look like a fool, Kathy thought, begging for clarification. So she just kept taking it in, trying to sort it out.

That spring was also the time of being pestered to death about turning sixteen and showing no interest in driving. This wasn't *normal*, her parents decided. Normal was heading down to take your test on your birthday, like Kenny.

"Actually, I blew the parallel parking," he admitted, "but somehow the guy didn't count it against me."

Honestly, life was so easy for Kenny, Kathy thought. People held up hoops, he jumped. He never wasted energy asking why, or wondering if the hoop shouldn't be a shade more to the left. Sometimes he simply smiled and the hoop holder, charmed, lowered it.

Kathy finally took the written test for her learner's permit, and sat in driver's ed watching movies of mangled bodies being pried from smashed cars, gore utterly wasted on her. These were films for people who never thought bad things could happen to them. Kathy always thought bad things *could* happen to her. Bad things *and* good things. All kinds of stories formed in her mind way too easily, like the one about how sorry

47

her parents would be if she got in an accident after they practically forced her into the driver's seat.

You were supposed to love cars, and she didn't. They were modern and unromantic. No wonder folk songs stuck to horses and trains. Besides, cars caused air pollution.

"That doesn't bother you when you drive around with Julia," Mom pointed out. "Really. That great big fancy car."

"But Mom, she hates it. She calls it the Toad-mobile."

"Wonderful. She gets the fun of driving it and sneering at it at the same time."

"Oh, Mom."

"You know, Kenny's told us some stories about this drama bunch that we find . . . a little upsetting. Frankly, we worry about drugs."

"I'm not doing drugs."

"I know, honey, and we trust you. But even the idea of hanging around people who do . . ."

"Nobody's smoking marijuana backstage, if that's what you're thinking." No need to mention that people hinted at smoking it everyplace else.

"Well, I hate to seem like a worrywart, but last week at bridge club, Marge Johnson said she'd heard that wearing one of those little brass bells means a person has tried LSD. And then when you come in with one a couple days later . . ."

"This?" Kathy pulled out the leather thong with the bell. "Hey, you're the one who thought I needed to accessorize!"

"Kathy."

"Mom, I haven't tried LSD. And I'm not going to, okay? Val just gave me the bell. It doesn't mean anything. You shouldn't listen to everything they say at bridge club. Don't listen to Kenny, either. I could tell you just as many stories about the jocks and the soshes. They're the ones you always hear bragging how drunk they got over the weekend."

"That's a little different, though. It's not illegal."

"Mom! It is if you're sixteen."

"Well, yes," she admitted, leaving unsaid what Kathy understood to be true. Alcohol was familiar. Drugs were scary and new.

Her parents would have been reassured to understand how little drugs appealed to her. But why should they have the luxury of reassurance when she still had to hassle the whole issue?

"Grass makes you feel amazing," David would say to her, eyes bugged behind his glasses. "You shouldn't knock it if you haven't tried it. And it makes you so creative." He offered as evidence a recent poem written under the influence. "Oh man, I was so stoned when I did this."

Peering at the lines of his stingy, psychologically suspicious handwriting, Kathy believed it. When she didn't respond quickly enough, he snatched the paper back.

"You're probably not sensitive enough to appreciate it," he said.

Maybe you had to be stoned to read it too?

CHAPTER

8

"YOU CAN RELAX now," Kathy told her mother, coming in from her final summer typing class. "It's official. I can type. Now it won't matter if no one marries me like you keep threatening."

"Kathy. I never said that." Her mother stirred a bubbling vat of raspberry jam. "You're the one who doesn't want to be a housewife. What's so criminal about encouraging you to get some practical skills to fall back on?"

"Right!" Kathy clenched a gung ho fist. "Just think—now, no matter what life hands me, I will always have this incredible skill to buck me up!"

Her mother sighed and pushed a loose strand of hair from her forehead with the back of her wrist.

"Here." Kathy handed over her certificate. "See? Fastest in the class."

"Really? That's great!"

"No, it isn't. It's compulsive. 'Anything worth doing at all is worth doing well.' You guys have certainly got that drilled into me."

She went to the refrigerator, thinking that even if

typing was faster than writing by hand, she still intended, on principle, to leave her typewriter under her desk.

"Now, I'm not sure if this is good news or bad," her mother said, "but you got something in the mail. From *Seventeen*? Your portfolio."

Kathy slammed the fridge. "Where is it?"

"In the living room." Her mother eased the vat off the burner and followed her.

Kathy's pulse pounded. She started ripping. "Oh, please please please," she moaned. "Let me be a finalist." She fished out a letter, which she scanned, then dropped with a wail.

"What does it say?"

"It says, 'Thanks for entering, sucker!'"

"Kathy, they probably had thousands of girls entering. Anyway, what do those judges know? I think your pictures are terrific."

"You just say that because you're my mother." She went into her bedroom and threw herself across the bed. "Now I'm never going to be an artist!"

Her mother sat down next to her. "Why not? You're not going to let one bunch of judges stop you, are you?"

"Oh, right. 'If at first you don't succeed, try, try again.'"

"I know it's disappointing . . ."

Kathy flung around to face her mother. "Oh no, Mom, nothing can disappoint me. After all, remember, I know how to type!"

CHAPTER
9

HAPPY HOUR STARTED as soon as Kathy's family and her parents' friends the Palmers had beached their boats at the far end of Cultus Lake. The Shays had survived the usual vacation concerns: the car overheating as it pulled the trailered motorboat and gear over Santiam Pass, the hassle of piloting it—little sailboat in tow—to the far end of the lake, the anxious quest to secure the perfect campsite.

By the time the tents were up and the smell of steaks on the grill filled the air, all four adults were sipping their second gin and tonics and feeling no pain.

After dinner, campfires dotted the lake's crescent cove; music blared from a camp three sites down.

"I'll bet they're the ones with the cute boys," Mom said.

"You know who they are, don't you?" Marilyn Palmer said. "Family that owns all the Handyman Hardware Stores."

"Oh. Interesting," Mom said. "Kathy, you and Christie ought to go check this out."

"Mom."

"Kenny can go with you."

But Kenny was watching Christie Palmer with newfound interest. He had his pop, his Fritos. He had no incentive to move.

"Want to?" Christie said to Kathy. "Go down there?" Christie was the twins' age, and they'd always gotten along well enough on these two-family camping vacations, but maybe she and Kathy weren't as much alike as they used to be. Christie was blond and dimpled and somehow cuter than Kathy remembered from a year ago, a transformation not lost on Kenny either, judging from his vaguely goofy look.

"Come on, Kathy," her mother said. "Take a little walk down the beach. What else are you going to do? Just sit here?"

"I'm not just sitting. I'm reading." She held up *Wuthering Heights.* "Or trying to."

"Well, I'm not going if she isn't," Christie said.

The two mothers shook their heads at each other.

"I'll tell you, Marilyn," Mom said, "we never would have passed up a chance like this at their age, would we?"

That's how you ended up married at nineteen, Kathy thought.

"It's getting too dark to read anyway, Kathy," Mom said. "Why don't you get out your guitar?"

"Mom . . ."

"Come on, it'll be fun."

Fun. Her mother just wanted their campfire to look the liveliest, the most enviable. To her, a guitar was simply the correct accessory to include in a *Sunset Magazine* photo—"Campfire at Cultus Lake." She

53

thought this vacation was *her* story. She wanted Kathy to do her role the way *she* was making it up.

Kathy got her guitar out of the tent and, sitting on a stump, tuned it briefly.

"And now," Kenny said, "fresh from her world tour, Chintimini High's very own Maid of Constant Sorrow, Kathy Shay!"

Christie giggled appreciatively.

"How about one of your pretty folk songs?" Mom said.

"Scarborough Fair"? "Black Is the Color"? No, too tame. Kathy commenced with the rhythmic thrumming of "Anathea," a ballad from her Judy Collins album about a girl who sacrifices her virginity to a judge in a desperate effort to save her brother from the gallows.

When the song ended with the warning that Anathea would find her brother in the woods, hanging, Marilyn turned to Kathy's mother.

"Doesn't she know anything cheerful?"

Mom brightened. "How about 'I've Been Workin' on the Railroad'? We can do that without the guitar."

Dad and Ross Palmer joined in, hearty and hokey—while Kenny and Christie inched down in their lawn chairs with embarrassed little snorts. Kathy glanced over her shoulder. Were the people in the next camp watching?

"How about another one, Kathy?" Ross said when they were done. "If you think you're going to be a professional folksinger, you're going to have to sing in front of people without making them beg."

Kathy shot her mother a glance, then started her fanciest picking combination. She was not going to be a folksinger. She'd never actually come out and admitted that yet, but somehow she knew it was true. She began to sing:

> *"Oh, the rivers never will run dry*
> *Or the rocks melt with the sun*
> *I'll never prove false to the boy I love*
> *Till all . . . all these things be done . . ."*

Maybe it wasn't the music of these songs she'd always loved so much anyway. Maybe it was the words.

"So you have a boyfriend now?" Christie said under her breath when Kathy had finished "Fare Thee Well."

"No. What makes you think that?"

"Well, the way you sang that. It sounded—"

"I don't," Kathy said flatly, feeling found out somehow. That her longing, her love and loyalty for the boy she hadn't even met yet should be so obvious . . .

"Hey," Christie said, "do you know 'Ode to Billy Joe'?"

Kathy shook her head. "I'm not into that hit parade stuff."

"Oh, I love that song," Christie said. "It just makes you *wonder*, you know? I mean, what *were* Billy Joe McAllister and his girlfriend throwing off the Tallahatchee Bridge? I could think about that for hours."

Kathy regarded her through half-lowered lashes. "You could?"

"Kathy." A cautionary look from her mom.

"Did you ever think maybe Bobbie Gentry didn't even know herself when she wrote that?" Kathy said. "Maybe she just left it hanging so everyone would go, whoa! Weird!"

Christie's eyes were big. "But they had to throw *something* off."

"No, they didn't."

"But it says—"

"It's a *story*, Christie. It's made up."

She launched into Dylan's "Masters of War," chiding the older generation for ruining the world with war plots and scaring people so bad about the future that pretty soon they wouldn't even dare have babies.

"You let her sing that crap?" Ross said before the final harsh chord had faded.

"Ross!" Marilyn said.

"You know, it's this music that's got the kids all screwed up. Listen to the goddamn lyrics! When those Rolling Stones creeps got away with doing that song on TV I said that's it, no more Ed Sullivan in *this* house. I don't care if they did change the words. Everybody knew it was something about spending the night together. Honest to God, these kids preaching free love, lousing up their genes with LSD, squawking about the service. Spoiled brats. Army'd be the best thing for 'em. Say what you will, those war years were the best of our lives."

Kathy glanced at her mother and Marilyn. Didn't they hear the insult in this? One thing for sure, she thought. I won't stand for a husband who has to keep insisting his best years were the ones he spent apart from me. Or at least he better not say so all the time.

But the two women just gazed, hypnotized, into the coals and started singing all the old sentimental songs, the music from those war years when everyone was swept up in the dream of marrying their

56

returning sailors and soldiers. "As Time Goes By" . . .
"We'll Meet Again" . . .

World War II. As a little girl, Kathy had pictured
the entire population of the world—men, women,
and children—divided into two sides, squaring off
with quarterstaffs. Even after television taught her
about tanks and bombs, that war still seemed so much
simpler than Vietnam. Good guys versus the bad
guys, and they could all feel proud America had won.

The campfire burned low, and in the satin stillness
of the lake, the reflected stars hung suspended. Dad
and Ross stood at the water's gravelly edge, the orange
lights of their cigarettes arcing up and down.

"There'll be bluebirds over . . ."

Oh no, "The White Cliffs of Dover." Tonight,
somehow, this one got to Kathy worse than ever. To
think of the poor guy who wrote it, scratching out
these hopeful lines about life after the war—love and
laughter and peace ever after—never guessing that
somewhere, right at that instant, men were feverishly
developing the nuclear bomb.

CHAPTER
10

"WE'RE BUZZING OVER to the lodge for ice," Kathy's father said. "Anybody want to add anything to the list? You want a paper, Jeannie?"

"No. Thank. You," Mom said. "This is vacation. I do not want to know what's happening out there."

Kathy raised her cheek from the fragrant straw mat and propped her chin on her hands. You could bet the war in Vietnam was still going on. And now they had fighting at home. Newark and Detroit had been in flames a few weeks earlier. People had actually died in the rioting. But here in the clear mountain air, where time was measured only by the sun, cities as they knew them were hard to remember; cities ablaze were inconceivable. And that was the way her parents wanted it. Even if the reception had been decent—which it wasn't—they wouldn't have brought a radio.

Her father, in particular, had amazing faith in the protective powers of the wilderness and its remoteness. "If they ever drop the bomb," he said once, "we'll just gather up everybody we care about and head into the mountains." Had he ever heard of fallout? Kathy remembered wondering. Did he really picture himself thigh deep in a rushing stream, casting his fly rod as the world burned to cinders? The end of civilization as an extended backpacking trip? She imagined them all standing together at a viewpoint, watching the mushroom clouds rising from the valley towns below. "Just remember," he would intone, "every cloud has a silver lining . . ."

"How are we doing for suntan lotion?" Mom said.

Marilyn looked up from her paperback copy of *Valley of the Dolls* and gave her tube a test squeeze. "Better get some more."

Marilyn sported a plaid two-piece suit cut clear below her navel. Mom seemed impressed that her friend's stomach was still flat enough to get away with this, but Kathy was glad her own mother wore a one-piece. Marilyn had to be almost forty, after all. Kathy made a mental note never to try to look young when she wasn't anymore.

Christie's suit was the smallest of all, an actual bikini. One time Kathy caught her father and Ross watching her wade into the lake, shaking their heads in wonderment at her new curves.

"That doesn't seem right," Kathy told her mother later. "Dads shouldn't be checking out their daughters' figures. Do you think?"

"Well, she's there. She's lovely. How could any of us not notice?"

"Still . . . ," Kathy said. Nobody seemed to be looking at her like that. And she had an okay body, didn't she? Not fat. Not skinny. But Christie . . . oh shoot, it was amazing how much stir that extra nice little curve at her waist seemed to cause, the way her hips rounded out.

The next time Kathy's father wanted to boat over to the lodge, Mom insisted Kathy go too. At the lodge dock, instead of getting out after cutting the motor, Dad started hedging around about what men found attractive in girls.

Uh-oh—a prearranged heart-to-heart. Why did Mom always do this?

"Sometimes," he said, "the way you hear guys talk, you might get the idea that all we care about is a girl's figure."

"It's okay, Dad." Obviously Mom had reported to him the entire Christie-in-a-bikini conversation, and he was working from some imagined "good father" script.

"Now, I'm not going to deny that's important. It's nature, after all. It's the way we're made."

"Dad, really. You don't have to apologize."

"I know, but you need to realize there are other things far more important. Any guy who would go for a gal based only on her dynamite figure would just be a jerk—in my book, anyway."

Kathy nodded, wondering exactly what Mom had suggested he say.

"In fact," Dad was going on, "it's usually not the figure that attracts the guy at all."

"It's not?" Here it comes, the big fairy tale about deep down, guys admiring brains.

"No, not at all," her father said. "I'd say, nine times out of ten, believe it or not, what most attracts a guy is—a pretty face."

ON THE FOURTH day, Kenny suggested they take the little sailboat over and check out the next cove. Kathy declined in favor of *The Hunchback of Notre-Dame*, but Christie jumped at the invitation.

They were gone for two hours. The moms had just started making noises about hiking around to find them when the little blue boat came bobbing out from behind the point.

After that, Christie and Kenny were together practically every minute, giggling and goofing off, taking long moonlight walks down to the deserted end of the beach, where they did who knows what.

But the parents didn't seem concerned. Mom actually acted as if she approved, and kept making wistful comments about summer romances.

Summer romance. How could you stand to fall in love, Kathy wondered, if you knew there was a fixed end to it?

She found herself making up stories for herself featuring a new character—the true love she would never betray, a boy who would show up when school started again and immediately like her better than all the dimpled cheerleaders put together. He would realize she wasn't cranky, she was . . . deep.

One afternoon she took the little sailboat out on her own. Inadvertently letting a gust catch the sail wrong, she dumped herself into the cold, choppy water. A huge motorboat roared to the scene and in short order she was being pulled aboard by two of the Handyman Hardware boys. Draping a towel around her, they asked over and over, "Sure you're okay?"

She kept nodding, a little surprised at how nice those big hands around her upper arms had felt. As they righted her boat, she glanced back toward shore. Everyone at her camp would be taking in this little drama. Christie would probably think she'd tipped the boat in front of the boys' camp on purpose. She'd be wondering whether Kathy could play her cards right, now that she had this golden opportunity.

After they exchanged names and started the slow tow back to the beach, the blond one (Blake? Or was he Drake?) said, "So what do you do for fun?"

"Well . . ." She pulled the towel tight around her. "That's hard to say." She didn't feel like saying "singing" anymore.

"Come on." He grinned. Very nice teeth.

"Um, I like painting sets. You know, for stage plays?"

They looked at each other, then back at her. "No, we mean for fun."

"It *is* fun."

The brown-haired one smirked. "Sounds like work to me."

"Well, it is, but it's fun too."

They looked at each other again. Work as fun. What a concept. Yuk yuk yuk.

"Maybe *fun*'s the wrong word," she said, feeling a blush rise. "It's very . . . satisfying."

"Satisfying?" This was even funnier.

"So what do *you* do?" she asked.

"I don't think we better tell you, do you, Blake?"

"Hey, what about the blonde at your camp? Drake here's got a thing for her."

"Hey, man, so do you!"

By the time they were back to shore and the boys vaulted out into the shallows to pull the sailboat in, Christie was posed there in her bikini, waiting.

CHAPTER
11

KENNY SWUNG AROUND the doorjamb of Kathy's room. "Ready to go?"

"Not hungry yet." She sprawled across her bed, reading. "You?"

"Duh. Would I be asking?"

Kathy sighed. When Mom and Dad had first announced plans for going out this evening, Mom had guilt-tripped her. What a shame, how she'd always sidestepped cooking! What a nice opportunity this would have been to practice on Kenny.

"Mom. How come it's not a shame Kenny can't cook for me?"

"Oh, Kathy." Silly, obviously.

"No, I mean it. How come you never hassle him about learning to cook?"

"Actually, I think it would be a good idea if he did." Said with the pride of the enlightened. "There'll always be times when it would come in handy."

Like when his wife was busy giving birth or something? Exactly the level of culinary skill Kathy herself aspired to—just competent enough to avert starvation if no one more enthusiastic appeared to prepare the food.

"Couldn't we just throw in chicken pot pies?" Kathy said to Kenny now.

"Come on! Three tacos and a drink. Dinner for a dollar. Can't beat that."

"Oh, all right."

"Hey, what's that?" he said, indicating her booklet.

"Script for *The Crucible*. The fall play?"

He looked doubtful. "What's a crucible, anyway?"

"Well, it's like a test."

"Like SATs? You're doing a play about SATs?"

"Ha ha." She tossed the script aside. "It's like a very difficult moral test. The play's about the Salem witch trials."

"Great. Who's gonna be the head witch? Julia McCullough?"

"Kenny! Look, if you're going to be this way, I don't even want to go with you."

"Hey, I'm just showing an interest. Anyway, Mom gave me the dinner money." He held up two dollars. "And I'm the one with the driver's license."

"Oh, all right then, let's go." She marched out to the car.

"I'm doing you a favor," he said, following. "You wouldn't want people knowing you're the last person in town to try tacos."

"I've eaten tacos."

"Yeah, when?"

"I don't know. At the Seattle World's Fair? Or didn't Mom make them once?"

"That doesn't count. I mean real tacos. Taco Bell tacos."

"Whatever you say." She rolled down her window

to let her hair stream out. Eating was just something you had to stop and do every once in a while so you could get on with whatever else you were trying to accomplish.

"So tell me more about the play," Kenny said.

"Like you care."

"Come on, Kath. I'm sorry. I shouldn't make fun."

She eyed him warily. "Well, Arthur Miller wrote this in the early fifties, see? At the time of the McCarthy trials, when everybody was accusing everybody else of being Communists. All somebody had to do was say you were a Red and you'd lose your job and your life would be wrecked."

"Whoa," Kenny said.

"Same thing with the witch trials. These girls got all turned on about having the power to condemn people as witches. And it was tricky, see, because if you confessed to being a witch they hung you, but if you didn't, they killed you too."

"Hey, that's nuts."

"I know, but it really happened. Anyway, it's a terrific play. It was on TV with Tuesday Weld as the girls' ringleader, Abigail."

"So that's the part you want?"

"No, that'll be Julia, probably. I want to be Mary Warren. She's kind of timid, but she tries to tell the truth in court. Then Abigail scares her into going along, so she freaks out."

Kenny nodded. "Sort of a peer group pressure story."

"Well, yeah, I guess it is." She grimaced. "Oh, I hope I get the part."

"You probably will. You know the blind girl thing

last year? I heard lots of kids saying you should have got that."

"You did? Kenny, why didn't you *tell* me?"

"I don't know. I didn't think you cared what I had to say." He turned into the fake-mission-style restaurant. "Taco Bell! Boy, I could eat here every night!"

"HOW INTERESTING," JULIA whispered as they came down the sloped aisle of the auditorium. "James Holderread. Suppose he's trying out?"

"Where?" Kathy scanned the clusters of students.

"There, in front. Sitting by himself. I thought he was only into politics or whatever."

"I wonder if he's any good," David said. "I think he's too short, don't you?"

"Too short for what?" Kathy said.

"Well, for the lead, of course. John Proctor. *My* part."

"Stop obsessing, will you?" Julia said. "You're going to be John Proctor. Anyway, you know we never have enough boys trying out. I hope Holderread *is* good. Even if he is sort of—well, on an ego trip." She turned to Kathy. "Don't you think?"

"I guess." Kathy had heard he was super-smart. "He's in my American history class this term but I don't know him that well." She craned for a glimpse. She couldn't help being impressed that, unlike her, he apparently hadn't felt it necessary to drag along a friend for support.

Mr. Corwin got up and talked about the play itself and finished with his usual don't-be-nervous speech.

Right. Kathy took a deep breath. She'd studied the

script. She'd done the ritual hair washing and worn her current favorite outfit—black Mary Janes and tights, Lanz skirt with the embroidered waistband, a white, Victorian-collared blouse. She had even practiced shrieking in the shower. She was as ready as she'd ever be, but her stomach felt awful.

Oh, to be like Julia, who sat with half-lowered eyelids, bored and blasé as a jet-setter ignoring the stewardess's emergency landing instructions.

AN HOUR INTO tryouts, the vice principal made an entrance and whispered something to Mr. Corwin.

"Okay," Mr. Corwin announced, turning, "that's going to be it for today. We've got a windstorm kicking up and everybody has to head home."

A collective groan.

"Sorry, but we've got power outages and trees falling. If anything's going to happen to you jokers, the administration wants to make sure it doesn't happen on school property."

"We'll drive you home," Julia said to Kathy. "I've got the Toadmobile."

Kathy followed Julia and David out to the student parking lot. Pulling onto Pierce Street, they spotted James Holderread leaving on foot.

"I should give him a ride," Julia said.

"Julia!" David said. "He's after my part!"

"So? Giving him a ride isn't giving him the part. What do you think, Kathy?"

In the backseat, Kathy shrugged. James looked rather dramatic, plowing coatless into the wind, his dark hair wild. Branches flailed, twigs rained around him.

Julia braked. Kathy opened the back door.

"Uh, want a ride?" Kathy said.

He hesitated, squinting at the sky. "I like storms."

She hesitated. "So do I."

They looked at each other.

"Could we discuss this amazing coincidence," David said, "with the door closed and the car moving forward?"

James dropped in beside Kathy. He was wearing jeans and a blue work shirt—what he wore every single day, now she thought of it.

"Ever wonder if you're some sort of jinx?" Julia said to James, accelerating.

"Huh?"

"Every time you show up for something, it gets canceled. The hootenanny?"

"Oh." He laughed shortly. "Yeah."

The ill-fated hootenanny seemed ages ago. The possibility of another had never come up. Hootenannies were out. Now even the word made Kathy cringe. Just as well she'd figured out her voice probably wasn't good enough for a real singing career. Saying you wanted to be a folksinger was starting to sound a little hokey.

"Camel?" Julia said, and David lit her one.

James promptly rolled down his window. Kathy flicked him a grateful glance.

They drove on in silence. Without James in the car, the other three would probably have been analyzing the initial tryouts. But James was an outsider. James was competition. Kathy felt incredibly conscious of his blue-jeaned thigh just inches from hers.

"Isn't Diane ever going to try out again?" Julia finally asked. Maybe this seemed like a safe subject.

"I doubt it," Kathy said. "And after what happened last year, I'm sure not about to encourage her."

Julia took a puff on her cigarette. "I'm so disappointed in her. Really, Steve Landers . . ."

"Yeah." Kathy might have said more if James hadn't been hearing this. After all these years, Diane had given up sharing lockers with Kathy so she could share with Steve. And whenever Kathy tried to talk to her, he was there like a guard, as if Kathy were some kind of contagious disease he was determined to keep Diane from contracting.

James's house turned out to be an enchanted Tudor cottage, complete with leaded windows—not the usual in a town of ranch-style tract homes.

"How'd you know where he lives?" Kathy asked Julia after James got out.

"Well, we did go to the same junior high. God, look at the wind."

But Kathy was watching James as he loped off toward his round-topped, iron-hinged front door.

"YOU PROMISED *I'D* be John Proctor!" David complained to Julia the morning after final tryouts when they checked the cast list.

"When I said that," Julia whispered, "we hadn't heard James read, had we?"

"Julia!"

"Well, he *was* awfully good. And anyway, Judge Danforth is an important part too."

All this swirled around Kathy, who stood dazed and delighted. She'd been cast as Mary Warren!

Julia laid a protective hand on her shoulder. "Congratulations, little one."

As James Holderread approached the list, the

group fell silent. They watched as he checked it and then, without any visible reaction, walked away.

But just before he rounded the corner at the end of the hall, he glanced back at them. Kathy smiled, just a flash: Hey, look, we're both winners.

His fingers formed the peace sign. Or was it *V* for *Victory?*

CHAPTER
12

"WHAT DO YOU think?" Kathy's mom said, parking at the main gate of the Willamette University campus in Salem. "Do you want to get out?"

This long-planned college campus tour had already taken the two of them through Lewis and Clark in Portland, Pacific University in Forest Grove, and Linfield in McMinnville. The sweeping lawns, stately trees, and red brick buildings were all starting to blend together in Kathy's mind.

"Let's walk around," her mother said, "while the sun's out."

Kathy sighed and pushed open the car door.

"You always loved the golden pioneer," her mother said, looking up at the statue topping the state capitol across the street.

"Uh-huh," Kathy agreed, wondering just how much this was supposed to weigh in the university's favor.

Down yet another rain-washed walkway, she trailed her mother's clicking heels. *Heels,* if you could believe it. And one of her knit suits.

"Well," Mom said, "what do you think?"

Kathy looked around. "It's a campus."

"Oh, come on. Is that all you can say?"

What *should* she say? The whole thing hurt her brain. Important Decisions About Your Future! False Steps May Prove Disastrous!

"Well," she said tentatively, "I like those turret things on that building. The big sequoias are . . . impressive."

"Yes . . . ?"

"Hey, I'm sorry. Like I said back at Linfield, I'm really not sure what we're supposed to be able to tell just by looking at a lot of green grass."

"We're trying to get a feel for the place, honey. You know, intuition. See if you can imagine yourself here."

Kathy watched her mother lift her face and inhale. Clearly *she* could picture herself here.

"As I said when we started out," her mother went on, "no matter how much we study the catalogs at home, actually being on campus is better. We can . . . we can pick up on the vibes!"

Kathy sighed. Okay, so she'd try to give this place a fair going-over.

The students here seemed a shade too straight, she decided. They'd probably been the smart soshes at their high schools. In a few years they'd be government employees and lawyers.

She did see an intriguing bunch clustered at a doorway, but when one of the girls gave her a look of friendly interest, Kathy blushed miserably. What could be more embarrassing than being seen with a mother-type woman in a knit suit?

They continued through the campus, Kathy always a step or two behind.

"Well, this is certainly very nice," her mother said when they came to a pretty stream, "but I think I can see you best at Lewis and Clark."

"Did you notice the lady in the Lewis and Clark office had pierced ears?" Kathy said.

"Did she? I was busy noticing that other woman, the one with her son. That beige suit looked so . . . I don't know . . . classy. But anyway, didn't you think the Lewis and Clark theater department sounded good?"

"I guess."

"Seeing the kids there, somehow I thought you'd fit right in. And you know, I have to laugh when I remember saying you looked like a peasant washerwoman when you started parting you hair in the middle like that. Now practically every girl around does! I guess I've gotten used to it. Well, long, clean, shining hair is certainly prettier than those beehive things the girls were doing before."

Kathy swung back her hair, which now almost touched her waist. She'd wanted to be different. Now lots of people had long hair. Still, she wasn't about to cut it off just to make a point.

"Did you notice that cute blond boy back there," Mom asked, "how he looked at you?"

"Mo-om!"

"I wish you'd smile more. You look so pretty when you smile."

Kathy frowned. "Is this about education or mating?" But she couldn't help glancing behind her. She'd written off the boy's look as a product of her own hopeful imagination, but she was certainly willing to be wrong.

"Of *course* this is about your education," her mother said. "Oh, just think of all the learning going on in those buildings. Sometimes I think college is wasted on the young."

"So why don't you go back? What's stopping you?"

"Ha! You get married and have kids and then ask me that question."

"Maybe I don't want to get married and have kids."

Her mother stopped walking. "Okay, then— don't."

"Hey, I'm sorry, but you make it sound so depressing."

"I give up," Mom said. "Let's go get something to eat."

Kathy followed her back to the car. Why did she have to act like motherhood ruled out everything else? Did it? When you looked around at men, you didn't just see dads. Why was it so hard to find women who weren't just moms? And if being a mother meant you couldn't do anything else, why go to college at all?

THEY SLID INTO a booth by the coffee-shop window and ordered pie à la mode.

"Aren't all these colleges we've looked at really expensive?" Kathy said. "I don't want to bankrupt you guys."

"Don't worry, we'll manage. I really think a small private school would be best for you. I don't want you to get lost in the crowd."

The campuses they'd visited all seemed so quiet. Maybe that was the point. Her parents wanted her someplace safe, someplace unlikely to be the site of big antiwar riots. All the free-speech demonstrations at Berkeley had upset her father no end. What was the point of scraping together college money for your kids if they were going to spend all their time screaming in the streets?

Kenny, of course, could go to a big state school, whichever one would take him with his cheerfully mediocre academic record. The only crowds he'd ever find himself in would be at the football stadium, and no matter how many people there were, he wouldn't be lost. The point was simply to get him enrolled so he'd be safe from the draft.

Her mother checked her watch. "Maybe you ought to do the driving on the way home."

"No, thanks."

"Kathy, you're never going to get your license if we don't practice."

"All *right*."

Kathy's gaze drifted around the coffee shop. At one table, a middle-aged woman sat alone, eating a humble meal of soup and sandwich.

Kathy abruptly averted her eyes, staring down at her half-eaten marionberry pie. "I can't stand it."

"What? Is your pie bad? Mine's good."

"No, no. It's nothing."

"Honey, what is it?"

"Oh, that woman over there," she whispered. "I don't know. It just kills me."

Her mother turned around.

"Oh God, don't look!"

"What? What on earth is the matter?"

"Well, she's all alone. Just sitting in a restaurant eating soup by herself. That is the saddest thing."

Mom sighed. "Why? She's hungry; she's eating."

"But she's *alone.*" Should she really have to explain this? The world was full of sad, lonely people.

"Maybe she *wants* to be alone," Mom said, teeth set. "Maybe she has a bunch of teenagers at home and this is the first chance she's had to get away from them."

"Oh." Kathy looked at her and winced. "I'm awful, aren't I?"

Her mother didn't answer for a long time. Then she said. "I guess it's not easy being your age."

Kathy hung her head.

"Although I have to admit, when I was sixteen, I seem to recall having a lot of fun. I went to all the dances and games. And we had hayrides, and this one Valentine's dance I'll never forget . . ."

Kathy's eyes widened as the truth dawned—Mom had been a sosh! No wonder I'm such a disappointment, she thought.

"Do you think it's possible," Mom said, "that I'm not remembering things clearly?"

"No," Kathy said, "I'm sure you were having fun." She could easily imagine Kenny someday recounting his teen years in the same rosy terms. "You were probably born cheerful."

"And you were born gloomy?"

Kathy sighed. She hadn't been aware of being in a particularly bad mood. But look around, a world racked with war, cities in flames, the environment deteriorating moment by moment. To chirp around like a birdie in a Disney cartoon just didn't seem, frankly, like a very intelligent response.

They finished their pie in silence.

"All your dad and I ever wanted," Mom said, "was for you to be happy."

Kathy looked out the window. It was raining again. She turned back to her mother.

"Don't worry, Mom. I'll be okay."

CHAPTER
13

A FEW OF them had heard that Joan Baez had been arrested in California at the Oakland induction center, but the main subject of talk at Chintimini High was Julia. The incredible news ricocheted around the halls: Julia McCullough had split for Haight-Ashbury.

"This is so heavy," David said over and over.

"What did Mr. Corwin say?" Kathy asked him. "Has he heard?"

"Yeah. He didn't look happy, but he didn't exactly freak out. At least we're not that far into rehearsals."

"So how do you figure she got down there?"

"Hitched."

"David, that's so dangerous." A terrible story was already forming in Kathy's mind.

"Nah," David said. "Julia . . . she picks up people's vibes. She'd never get in a car with people who weren't mellow." He heaved a sigh. "God, Kath. What am I going to do? I mean, like, without her?"

* * *

THREE DAYS LATER the first San Francisco postcard arrived. David brought it to school, where it was passed around like a valuable artifact, evidence of a culture far away and exotic. Julia's psychedelic pen-and-ink drawing framed a legend: "Great things moving all the time here." The return address was a house number with a $^1/_2$ at the end. Kathy found this positively magical.

The cryptic postcards kept coming, addressed first to one friend, then the next, never the same return address twice. Winnie's read simply, "Mason City Street Fair."

San Francisco. Someone they personally knew was actually taking in the scene there, no doubt experiencing life on some higher level of consciousness than the rest of them.

"You got something from Julia," her mother said one day when Kathy came home after rehearsal.

Kathy snatched up the card. No real message, just drawings, with Julia's name in lowercase letters and a *p.s.* explaining she'd decided it was simply too pretentious for her to use capitals.

"Don't you love that?" Kathy's mother said, putting away groceries.

"What?" Kathy demanded.

"Oh . . . never mind."

"No, what? You read it?"

"Well, it's a *postcard*. How could I help it, sorting through everything? Besides, I know you don't think of it this way, but Julia is somebody's missing child. I wondered if there'd be a return address."

"She's not missing. She doesn't want to be found." The card, Kathy noticed, actually smelled like she imagined Haight-Ashbury would—a musty scent. "And it's my mail. It's private."

"If a person doesn't want something read, they shouldn't write it on a postcard. They've even invented a little device in case this becomes a problem. It's called an envelope."

"I hate it when you're sarcastic."

"Well, I don't appreciate you making it seem as if I'm snooping through your room or something."

"Mo-om."

"Which you know I would never do."

"All right, all right. But when it's mail in the pile, I still don't see why you can't take an attitude of . . . courteous indifference."

"Indifference? Ha! Just wait till you have a daughter of your own. Then we'll see how well you do at being indifferent." She stooped, pulling out saucepans, then stopped and turned, standing up. "*You're* not thinking of running away, are you?"

"No." Why get into her New York City fantasies? Besides, she always had trouble coming up with a credible scenario for a happy, post-running-away life. For starters, what would she do for money?

"I'm sure we would be absolutely devastated," her mother said. "You know, I ran into Arleta at Safeway. They just got back from San Francisco."

"Julia's parents went *down* there?"

"Well, of course they did. Turned the city upside down looking for her, just like I'm sure we would if it were you."

A picture formed in Kathy's mind, her parents wandering down Haight Street, desperation on their faces . . .

"I take it they didn't find her."

"No, and what they did find made them sick. Oh, Arleta was about to break down right there by the frozen TV dinners. Girls your age panhandling on the streets, kids out of their minds on drugs, sleeping on dirty mattresses laid wall-to-wall. They all go by nicknames and people hardly seem to know who lives in each apartment from one day to the next."

So which San Francisco was Julia in? The city of drugs and squalor? Or the city of flowers and love?

"AREN'T YOU WORRIED about her?" Kathy asked David backstage at rehearsal. "Not the hitchhiking. But when you hear about all this free-love stuff down there? You know, orgies and—"

"Orgies! Who've you been listening to? God, Kathy, you sound like some suburban society matron who wears hair rollers to bed."

"Well, pardon me. This isn't something I've made up, is it? The idea that people are sleeping around?"

"But it's all in how you look at it. If our parents' generation wants to make love sound dirty, that's their problem. We know love is beautiful. And beautiful things ought to be shared, right?"

Kathy squinted at him. "You're telling me you don't care if she decides to *share* with somebody besides you?"

"Hey, that would be strictly her business."

"Uh-huh."

"Really! I wouldn't mind at all!"

"Of course not."

"I mean, I certainly hope I could rise above the shallow values of the petty bourgeoisie."

Kathy flicked her hand, giving permission. "Rise away."

CHAPTER
14

KATHY WATCHED JAMES Holderread ease toward the front of the class and lean against the green chalkboard.

"All right, Mr. Holderread," the teacher said. "You may begin."

Straightening up, James riffled the edges of his index cards with his thumb. "I'd like to talk about the American Revolution," he began, and added with a smirk, "the first one, that is."

Gary Fry snorted.

He and James were rivals, famous for their hair-trigger eagerness to argue over the United States' presence in Vietnam.

Gary had been a proponent of the administration's position since junior high. Kathy remembered one argument after ninth-grade biology—Gary and a couple of his friends versus Enid Farley. Everyone knew Enid was weird, of course. You wondered if she ever washed her hair, and Gary said her parents were so far left, they were practically Communists.

Still, her insistence that the government had

manipulated people into thinking the U.S. was morally bound to send combat troops to Southeast Asia sounded credible, and Kathy had to admire her willingness to debate the issue when everyone knew boys didn't like girls who argued.

It even said so in the "becoming a woman" book her mother had given her. In a section called "A Boy Likes a Girl Who . . . ," one of the suggested traits was *Talks, but not too much or too loudly.* Ha! Now Kathy saw that book for what it was—part of a conspiracy to turn out a legion of housewife-mommy robots. Now she wished she'd had the guts to side with Enid. But no, she'd been busy studying that stupid list and trying to be a nice girl boys would like. And Gary had dumped her anyway!

She slouched in her seat, black-stockinged legs outstretched, ankles crossed. She was glad now. Who needed a jock-pack boyfriend who'd brag in the locker room about how far he'd gotten with you the night before? Stories about Gary's current conquests were certainly making the rounds. Lucky these stories weren't about her.

She folded her arms over her chest and settled back to listen to James's report.

Now that he was part of the drama group, she felt a certain camaraderie with him, and had begun to find him entertaining. You were always wondering what he'd do or say next.

When word had reached the administration offices that he would, as John Proctor, be roaring the word *whore* into the auditorium, the principal threatened to cancel *The Crucible*, producing cries of censorship and igniting free-speech protests. James wrote a blistering column for the school paper pointing out the ludicrousness of the jocks expressing outrage over a play they had no intention of attending. He managed to be funny, too, asking rhetorically whether they truly imagined the play would be enhanced by his changing Arthur Miller's *whore* line to "You're not a nice girl, Abigail! Not a nice girl at all!" In the end, the principal gave up.

Watching James now as he discussed the nature of revolution and the causes that led to the Revolutionary War, Kathy found him amazingly fluent. None of this um um um stuff you got from so many people. As he talked he made eye contact with each class member, working through his cards while barely glancing at them.

"In conclusion," he said, "I want to remind everyone how easy it is to think of history as something that happened way back when. We forget that history's being made all the time. Look what happened at the Pentagon yesterday, right? Revolution's the kind of thing that just might sneak up on you."

Kathy blinked, sorry he was finished. She'd been enjoying looking at him—that dimple in his chin, the little white jag of a scar through one black eyebrow.

"Well, Mr. Holderread," Mr. Plotkin said, "I must say, that was excellent."

"Thanks." James headed for his seat, cocky.

"What happened at the Pentagon yesterday?" somebody whispered.

"Big march," somebody whispered back.

"I can't say I hold with all your conclusions," Mr. Plotkin pointed out, "but you've done a good job of bringing it all together for examination. Now let's see . . ." He patted his desk blotter as if he'd lost something. "Oh, yes, Mr. Holderread, your index cards, please?"

"Uh, we have to turn them in?"

"Well, of course."

"But my writing's scribbly. You won't be able to read it."

"Just give me the cards, please. Quickly. We have several more reports to get through this morning."

James sighed and slouched toward the teacher's desk, rolling his eyes for the class's benefit as he handed the cards over.

Mr. Plotkin frowned. "Mr. Holderread, these are blank."

"Uh, yeah. That's why it doesn't make much sense to turn them in."

"The index cards were part of the assignment."

"Well, technically yes. You said to give a report using index cards." He hooked his thumbs in his pockets. "You never said the report had to be written on them."

Mr. Plotkin's face had gone red. "You realize this will count against you. Your grade, I mean."

"You're grading me down for not *needing* the cards?"

Kathy jumped up. "That's not fair!"

An outraged murmur of support surged around her.

"Excuse me, what does this have to do with you, Miss Shay?"

"Nothing, but I just don't think that's right. If he can give a good report *without* the cards, isn't that even better? You said yourself it was excellent."

"Your opinion, Miss Shay, is irrelevant. Sit down."

* * *

87

AND HE GAVE him a D!" Kathy concluded at the dinner table that night. "Can you believe it? It was the best report in the class. Everybody said so. Except Gary Fry, of course."

Her mother clucked. "Sounds like Mr. Plotkin has absolutely no sense of humor."

"Rules are rules," Dad said.

"But what's the point?" Mom said. "Obviously this boy went out and learned what he was supposed to. And I really think you have to pick your battles. This doesn't seem to me like one worth fighting."

"Why didn't Holderread just do the cards?" Kenny said.

"Kenny," Kathy said, "he didn't need to."

"Would have been easier to do it than fight about it."

"It's the principle, though. Just because *you'd* always take the easiest route."

"Yeah, well, what's so great about always wanting to stir things up?" Kenny said.

"Hey, if Plotkin hadn't made a big deal out of the cards, it wouldn't have stirred up anything."

"And Holderread would have been disappointed," Kenny said. "I'll bet he was deliberately trying to trick Plotkin."

"No, he wasn't!"

"How do you know?"

"Oh, stop it, you two," Mom said.

"Who is this kid, anyway?" Dad said.

"Well, James Holderread," Mom said. "Must be Richard Holderread's son."

"Who?"

Mom sighed. "Richard Holderread, at the university? He's in the English department."

"Makes sense," Dad said. "I should have known."

Kathy turned to him. "What's that supposed to mean?"

Dad pushed his chair back from the table. "It means I have to wonder about those guys. I saw a prof up by the campus the other day—he was wearing a turtleneck!"

"No!" Mom said in mock horror.

"I'm serious! I'm talking about a turtleneck with a tweed jacket—instead of a shirt and tie."

"How do you know it was a professor?" Mom said.

"Who else would pull a stunt like that?"

"Kathy, isn't James the one who got the hootenanny shut down last year?" Mom asked. "You said he was a show-off."

"Mom! Honestly, I wish you wouldn't do that."

"What?" She looked baffled. "What did I do now?"

"Well, that was way last year. Believe me, I remember perfectly well all the dumb things I've ever said without you always reminding me!"

CHAPTER
15

"THANKS FOR STICKING up for me in class," James said as they stood in the stage wings waiting for rehearsals to start. "You didn't have to."

"I know, but I couldn't help it, it just popped out. Mr. Plotkin makes me so mad."

"I thought it was funny."

"Yeah, still, you hate to have your grades wrecked."

"Oh, well. I filed a grievance."

"A grievance? What's that?"

"If you think a grade's unfair, you can complain."

"I didn't know that."

"Well, why would you? People with straight As don't have anything to contest."

"How do you know I have straight As?"

"You do, don't you?"

"Well, pretty close, but how do you know?"

He shrugged. "That's the usual when you take smart and add obsessive."

"Obsessive?"

"Sure. I've seen you taking notes in class, just ... *concentrating* so hard when Plotkin gives the assignment."

"Something wrong with that?"

He held up his hands defensively. "Hey, beats watching a girl doing her nails in class."

"I'm so glad you approve." She turned back to her script, trying to focus on her highlighted lines. But James was still standing right there, expectantly. "So what's the deal with you?" she said. "You get straight As *without* concentrating?"

"No, I *don't* get straight As. Grades are too subjective. And too many teachers have it in for me. But if a test is multiple choice or something, I make a point of getting a hundred percent. Then they can't argue." He grinned. "Makes 'em nuts."

Now why couldn't she be more like that? More devil-may-care.

"So what's a grievance?" she said, studying him out of the corner of her eye.

"Oh, yeah. Well, it's a way of getting your side of it down on paper. If colleges are looking through your transcripts, there'll at least be an explanation."

"You're not going to wind up with a D in the whole class, though."

"Right. But filing the grievance was kind of fun. Good practice."

"Practice for what?"

"Oh, I don't know . . . sticking up for myself against the system?"

THE FOLLOWING SATURDAY, James showed up at the set construction work party for the first time. When Kathy needed painting supplies downtown, he was the first to offer the use of his VW Bug.

"Can I ask you something personal?" she said as

91

they drove. "I've been wondering about that scar of yours. In your eyebrow?"

"Oh, this?" He rubbed a finger over his brow.

"Yeah. There's got to be a story behind that."

He laughed, his face going pink. "Naw, it's nothing. It's too dumb."

"Come on, *what?*"

He sighed. "Okay. Well. You know my friend Dan Weaver?" She nodded. Dan was one of the super-smart kids—chess, science, most likely to win a Nobel prize. "Couple of years ago he was trying to teach me to do 'Around the World'—you know, a yo-yo trick?"

"Oh, no! And you conked yourself?"

" 'Fraid so. Plastic. It splintered."

"Yow."

"You like that? Marked for life by a yo-yo. I'm not exactly proud of this, so don't go spreading it around, okay?"

At Kathy's father's store, she managed to slip in and put the paint on the school's tab without rousing her father from his office. She didn't want to field a bunch of questions about James at the dinner table that night.

Then James suggested they get coffee.

"James! You really drink coffee?"

He looked sheepish. "No. But I thought maybe you did."

She laughed. "Why?"

"I don't know, you just strike me as the sort of deep, dark serious person who probably drinks lots of black coffee."

"I do? Neat. But I'd rather have a shake."

"Hey, me too!" He started pawing through a

mess of receipts and old school papers in his glove compartment. "I thought I had a couple of bucks here."

"What's this?" Kathy pulled out a postcard—the Golden Gate Bridge. "From Julia! How come you didn't bring this to school?"

"What for?"

"Well, everybody else was."

"Yeah, so? Frankly, I wasn't all that impressed with her little exit."

"What do you mean?"

"Well, the way she let everybody down, quitting the play. How come you're all not pissed off?"

She looked at him in surprise. Maybe she'd been too busy feeling left behind to think about being mad. She scanned Julia's lines about the famous City Lights Bookstore and how she knew James, as a future great writer, would just love it.

"You're a future great writer?" she said.

"She wrote that, not me."

Kathy studied him, frowning. "You know, all she did was send you a postcard. You don't have to be so . . . annoyed."

"It's not the postcard. It's everybody going around, 'Oh, Julia, Julia!' all the time. 'Poor Julia, wonderful Julia, how can we ever live without Julia!' "

Kathy winced. "Is that how we sound?"

"Basically, yeah. And how do you think Siri Anderson must feel, trying to take over her part? What a pain, having to follow the great legend."

Kathy stuck the card back in the glove compartment. They were quiet as they turned onto Ninth Street.

"So," James said, "I s'pose now you don't want to share a shake with somebody who's not in the fan club, huh?"

"Oh, don't be dumb. Which do you like better? Seaton's or Custer's Drive-In?"

C H A P T E R
16

THE CRUCIBLE CAST bowed one final time, the curtain whooshed closed, and the Puritan girls burst into tears. In the huge group hug that followed, Kathy found herself pressed against James's fake leather vest.

"You were so good," he said.

"You too."

Later, after they'd struck the set and gathered for the cast party at Siri's, he brought his paper plate of chips and dip and sat beside her on the stairs.

"I really meant that," he said, "about you being a good actress. My parents thought you were best of everyone."

"Really?" Parental approval was so much more flattering when the parents weren't your own. "This is like the first real part I've ever had."

"Well, you must be a natural."

"A natural at hyperventilating and getting hysterical, maybe?"

"Somehow I think there's more to it than that."

"My parents thought you were good, too," she offered politely. Actually, her mother had said James seemed awfully "earnest," hinting at maybe *too* earnest. "I'll tell you, though," she'd added, "that kid is going to be one handsome man."

What a thing for a mother to say! And the idea of *going to be*. Interesting. Strange to remember, Kathy thought, that none of them were fixed in the present. Everyone was always in the process of becoming. But what a long time it seemed to be taking. And when would they know for sure just exactly what it was they were becoming?

Now she rubbed at a bit of greasepaint remaining between her fingers, surreptitiously watching James. He *was* good-looking—and somehow, mysteriously, he was looking better to her every passing minute.

"It's kind of a downer, isn't it?" she said. "The play being over."

"Yeah."

"I mean, opening night and closing night. You're up, then it's over. Two performances just aren't enough after all these rehearsals."

"Probably not, but I'm afraid everybody who wanted to see it already did."

"Isn't that pathetic? What did we have out there tonight? A hundred and fifty people?"

James shrugged. "You wouldn't have wanted the rest of those dimwits in the audience. They wouldn't have understood it anyway."

"That's true, isn't it?" She regarded him with new appreciation. "You know, I feel like I know you, the way we've been working on this all these weeks. But we haven't really talked much. I mean, with you being onstage practically the whole time . . ."

"Yeah."

"Think you'll try out again?"

"Maybe. But I doubt theater's going to be my thing."

She nodded. "You want to be a writer, right?"

"I guess. Or maybe I just say that to get my parents worked up."

"But isn't your dad in the English department? I'd think he'd like that."

"No, it's different, see. Being a teacher is practical, but saying you want to be a writer is going off half-cocked."

"I get that too!" she said, amazed.

"You do? But you don't want to be a writer, do you?"

"No, but I mean, it's the same thing. Every time I come up with something I like and it's creative, my parents go, 'That's nice, honey, you can be a music teacher or an art teacher.' And I'm going, Hey, I want to be the one actually singing the song, painting the picture, being up onstage, you know?"

"Yeah. Right. Exactly."

"I mean, here's my dad. He's so talented artistically, and it's just wasted, running an art supply store. Even the framing stuff is done by his employees, so he might just as well be selling . . . pet supplies. And look at Mr. Corwin, stuck here with us. He could have been a professional actor. Have you ever seen him do any of his stuff? He is so *funny*." She sighed. "I don't know, my parents think teaching is nice and safe and it's like their sacred parental duty or something to keep dragging me back to earth."

"I think you should be an actress," James said.

"Really?"

"Oh, yeah. Don't you?"

"Well, maybe. I hadn't really thought about it before, but I loved doing this show."

97

He nodded. "*My* parents keep saying I ought to be a lawyer. Born to argue, they call me."

She gave him a look. "You are kind of famous for that, aren't you?"

"Am I?"

"James! You *know* you are."

"Well, you're sort of famous for spouting off your mouth yourself."

"Am I?"

"I've seen your letters in the paper," James said. "Don't cut down the trees on Harrison Street—"

"Oh, no! I didn't know anybody at school read those!"

"Don't turn Central Park into a parking lot. Don't put the highway bypass by the river. And I like that one where you sort of told off the mayor."

"Really? Believe me, my folks weren't too thrilled. I was so worried about that after I'd mailed it."

"Why? All you did was say something that needed saying."

A slow smile spread over Kathy's face. What was going on here? Could it be? A Boy Likes a Girl Who Speaks Up?

Maybe there was hope. Maybe the author of that ridiculous "becoming-a-woman" book just forgot to interview anybody like James Holderread.

CHAPTER
17

KATHY LAY AWAKE for a long time that night, staring into the darkness. When had she ever talked so much to a boy? To anyone? They'd probably said more to each other in those two hours than she and Gary had in six months of "going steady."

They talked about their skepticism of groups, and how neither had ever been much of a joiner.

"Seems like as soon as you join a group," James said, "*any* group, everybody's supposed to think the same. If you don't, you get bad-vibed. I hate that."

"Oh, me too," Kathy said. "That herd mentality. I think that's why I never screamed for the Beatles. I might have liked them if nobody else had, but I couldn't stand the idea that every teenage girl was . . . well, *required* to go nuts."

James was serious, like her. He said he didn't go in for the concept of mindless hedonism. She agreed completely, and made a point of looking it up in the dictionary when she got home.

They talked about the war in Vietnam, a big deal with him. Sure, he said, he could evade the draft by getting into college and staying there, but was that right? To count on his privilege as a white, middle-class kid?

"Seems kind of cowardly," he said. "Maybe I should make more of a stand out of it—like go to jail."

"Would you really do that?"

"Maybe. I mean, you feel so powerless, just one person, but think about it: Without our bodies, those guys can't wage war. That's all there is to it. If *everybody* refused . . ."

He sounded so mature, Kathy thought, like he was twenty years old. She pictured them both that age, desperately clutching hands through prison bars.

James said his parents were ready to support him, whatever he decided.

She tried to explain how her folks tiptoed around the issue, avoiding argument. Her mother seemed more antiwar all the time, especially now that people like Dr. Spock, the trusted baby doctor, had started speaking out against U.S. policies. As for her father, he operated on the premise that he was a good American, and naturally thought what a good American should think—in this case, My country, right or wrong.

James told her he had two older sisters, already in college.

"I just have Kenny, my twin brother."

"Twin brother? You have a twin brother? Wait a minute. Not that Kenny Shay!"

"That's him."

"I can't believe it. I guess I should have figured it out, but you two seem so different."

"We are."

"So what's it like, being a twin?"

"I don't know. What's it like *not* being a twin? This is all I've ever known. And anyway, Kenny and I aren't very twinnish."

"You don't read each other's minds and stuff?"

"No."

"But always having somebody there . . ."

"Yeah. When we were little we were best friends. I mean, we fought, but we played together all the time too. It got kind of weird when girls started chasing him. I felt sort of . . . well, he was a pest but he was *mine*, you know? Except he wasn't. Now it's like we ignore each other at school and argue at home."

She lay in bed and thought back over all these things she and James had talked about, both of them going on and on about their families, friends, teachers.

"Mr. Sether's cool for English," he'd said. "In poetry last week he played Simon and Garfunkel songs and had us analyze the lyrics."

"Yeah? I like Simon and Garfunkel."

"Me too. Hey, did you know they're coming?"

"Here? To Chintimini?"

"Yeah," James said, "to the university."

"Oh my God, when?"

"March, I think. So, do you want to go?"

"Of course!" She looked at him. "Oh. You mean, with you?"

He laughed. "Yeah."

"Well, sure."

She couldn't believe it. March was months away. And he felt willing to plan something with her that far ahead?

Lying there, she thought about the clean line of his

jaw, the curl of his dark hair. Was it a sign of something, she wondered, when you wanted to describe what was probably one of the more ordinary eye colors as "the soft gray of a rainy Oregon sky"?

When she finally fell asleep, she seemed to be at the party still, in a cozy corner, talking to James. In the dream, though, they touched. In real life, they hadn't, not one brief brush of a hand. But if vibrations were visible, the air between them would have been white hot and flashing.

SHE DRIFTED THROUGH Sunday in the most mixed-up mood. *The Crucible* was over. Such a letdown. They would never do it again. The yellow roses her parents had sent to the dressing room were already looking sad and limp.

On the other hand, now there was James.

"Mom. Tell me again the story about the first time you saw Daddy. Did you just *know*, the minute you saw him?"

"I knew I thought he was cute."

"But you didn't know, like, Whoa, he's the love of my life."

"Well, maybe not instantly, no." She regarded Kathy with fresh interest. "Honey, what's going on? Are you thinking you're in love?"

"No! I mean, I don't know."

Could it happen like this? After all, she'd been aware of James for a whole year without any bells ringing. *Bells ringing.* What dumb song was that from? All her life she'd listened to songs and read stories and books, always looking for clues, answers to the big questions—Is this how life is? Is this how love is? Honestly, she thought, people ought to be very careful what they write and publish because some of us are believing every word!

Could a person be your true love without you recognizing it? Wasn't there supposed to be an awakening kiss or something? The hero sort of *informs* the heroine with this kiss? She looks startled as she pulls back and realizes, Wow, we're in love!

But wait a minute, maybe all these writers were just making this stuff up! Maybe it wasn't even their honest view of how life is. Maybe it was more like how they wished it would be. Maybe you had to watch your own life and just see for yourself how it all panned out.

Because so what if she and James had never kissed? So what if she'd halfway known him for a year without being struck by lightning? Maybe it didn't have to happen any certain way as long as it happened.

SHE STEPPED OFF the school bus Monday morning and crossed the patio on quaking knees. Could she have only imagined that some current had zapped between them Saturday night? Maybe her brain had concocted the whole preposterous idea from nothing, just made up one more story. Maybe they'd pass in the hall and those gray eyes would coolly sweep over her . . .

She reached the double doors, looked up.

There he was, just inside, waiting for her. He pushed open the door and held it.

Their eyes met.

Yes.

No mistake.

Something in his expression said he'd been drifting around for the last thirty hours just as she had—waiting, wondering, existing only for this moment.

"Hi," she said.

"Hi."

They stood there. Suddenly they laughed. At themselves, at each other, at the goofiness of the hopeful, lit-up, blissed-out smiles of recognition they now realized were spread across their mirrored faces.

We two, this look said, we are for each other.

CHAPTER 18

"WHAT A THING to have to hear through the grapevine," Diane complained, steering Kathy out of the streaming hall traffic into the drinking fountain alcove. "Weren't you ever going to tell me yourself?"

"Tell you what?"

"Don't play innocent. You and James Holderread, that's what."

Kathy blushed, enjoying the attention. Diane hadn't been interested in anything she'd had to say for months, it seemed, but a boyfriend—this was a different story.

"Well," Kathy started, "it happened really fast. We—"

"I can't get over it! James Holderread. I guess he is kind of cute, if you like that hippie look. And you *would* go for some broody brain type. Oh, I'm sorry, go ahead. Tell me everything!"

KATHY CRINGED WHEN she overheard her mother on the phone telling someone she and James were dating.

You didn't *date* your best friend, your soul mate. *Dating* made it sound so formal, as if you were doing that complicated dance of waiting for his phone calls, setting up each meeting. Kathy and James had to be together and they both knew it. What was to arrange?

When they couldn't be together, they got on the phone. What a thrill, picking up the receiver to his low, sweet voice. He always sounded so . . . intimate. They had an incredible amount of catching up to do, trading tales of everything that had happened in the first sixteen years of their lives.

For Kathy, James was like a favorite character in a book or movie. She loved picturing him in all the different scenes he described, imagining him as a little kid.

He insisted he'd been a smart-alecky brat, but she said that was okay, she'd been a smart-alecky, Goody Two-shoes sort of brat herself.

He told her about learning to write his name when he was barely four and how he couldn't understand why his parents weren't more excited when he scribbled it inside the front cover of every hardbound book they owned.

"When you're a famous writer," she said, "those books will be worth a fortune!"

They compared lists of all the books they'd ever read and found very little overlap. In grade school, while she was devouring *Little Women* and every other Louisa May Alcott, he was reading a Walter Brooks series.

"Freddy the Pig?" she said. "What on earth is that?"

"You haven't heard of Freddy the Pig? Hey, I'm sorry, but I'm not sure I want to associate with a girl who doesn't know Freddy the Pig."

"Come on, pig books?"

"Well, they're really about politics. The bad guys are always realtors or unscrupulous businessmen or pompous politicians."

His current list was completely intimidating— *Demian* by Hermann Hesse, Dostoyevsky's *The Possessed*, Cervantes's *Don Quixote*.

He admitted he'd liked a couple of girls in junior high, but he was shy, he said. He never let on and nothing happened. She told him about Gary Fry and relished his outrage at the part about the bonfire-date-turned-lecture.

"He did that?" James said. "Really? Geez, I've always thought he was a jerk, but that's— Wow, too bad I'm a pacifist. Makes me want to pop him one."

She loved comparing notes on what they'd first thought when they'd noticed each other at the hootenanny.

"You sang 'Black Is the Color,' " James said.

"Hey, that's right."

"I remember watching you, just . . . wishing you were singing about me."

"James! That's so strange, because in a way, I was." She explained how she'd planned on doing "Maid of Constant Sorrow," had to think of a new song, then caught sight of his black hair.

She loved this—their story, imagining it from the outside. These two people noticing each other, never knowing they'd one day fall in love.

"Actually," he confessed, "one of the reasons I tried out for *The Crucible* was that I'd seen you hanging around with that crowd."

"Really? But James, you never said one word to me all last year."

"I told you, I'm shy! I was afraid I'd blow it."

She admitted admiring the cleft in his chin; he insisted it was truly annoying to go around with this Dudley Do-Right feature. She also found endearing the little space between his two front teeth. This he appreciated. The dentist had wanted to wire his teeth to force it out, he said, but he refused. What did he care about conforming to some All-American smile standard?

She sat in class and dreamed of him, of being alone with him, parked down by the river in his green VW Bug. She no longer thought of cars as unromantic. She was even beginning to love the warm, cozy smell of aged vinyl.

This, she thought, is what all the songs were talking about.

She came home with flushed cheeks and tangled hair, which she hastily raked with fingers on the way from James's car to her porch. She drifted through the days, glowing in a way she couldn't hide no matter how nervous her parents' scrutinizing looks made her. "Whatever happened to that Maid of Constant Sorrow who used to hang around here?" they kept saying. Had they guessed what she and James were up to? Something more than a goodnight kiss?

Finally one day in a rare moment alone with Diane, Kathy mustered her courage.

"Can I ask you something, Diane? Something personal?"

"Sure."

"When Steve holds your hand, or . . . you know . . . kisses you, do you ever . . . get a certain feeling?"

"Well, yeah. I get all sorts of feelings."

"No, I mean, a real *specific* feeling." Honestly, why was this so hard? They were supposed to be the liberated generation, right? Their parents were the uptight ones. "A warm, buzzy feeling. In a certain place?"

"Oh." Diane's dark eyebrows went up knowingly. "Yeah."

Kathy studied her. "Are you sure you know what I'm talking about?"

Diane laughed, her little silver earrings shimmying. "You are so funny." Her eyes bugged out. "Yes! I know what you're talking about. It's perfectly normal, silly. You're *supposed* to feel that."

"Oh." Kathy blushed, all at once realizing Diane was way ahead of her on this. "Well, I just . . . I mean, the first time that happened. You know."

"Yeah, I know."

Finally, Kathy thought, life was starting.

CHAPTER
19

"JULIA'S BACK," WINNIE said, whipping by Kathy in the hall on the last day before Christmas vacation. "She's here. Now."

Kathy followed, half running. Outside, the sun was a ghostly disk showing through thin fog. At the curb, Julia stood talking to David, one palm propping her elbow, the other hand raised, holding a cigarette beside her pale face in a kind of benediction.

Seeing Kathy, she opened her arms, and they hugged, laughing.

"When did you get back?" Kathy asked breathlessly. Julia smelled of heavy musk, she noticed, the hippie scent of San Francisco.

"Oh, a couple days ago."

"Your parents found you?"

Julia made a face—ridiculous idea!—and then broke into a fit of coughing. "I just decided it was time to come back," she said when she recovered. "That's all."

"She's not coming back to school, though," David said.

Julia inhaled on the cigarette, coughed again until she was left swiping at teary eyes.

"Julia, are you okay?" Kathy said. "I mean, really okay? Because you don't look . . ."

Julia smiled sweetly. Too sweetly. "I don't look what?"

Kathy glanced away, embarrassed to be put on the spot. But good grief—Julia looked wasted. Didn't she realize that? You really had to wonder exactly what kind of life she'd been living down there.

"My parents are sending me to a private school in Portland," Julia said. "Oregon Episcopal? It's a boarding school."

Boarding school? Boarding schools were only in English novels, or on the East Coast. Schools for that same mysterious bunch who were shipped off to spend entire summers at camps in the Adirondacks.

"But why?" Kathy said.

Julia blew a wavery smoke ring. "My parents think people here are a bad influence on me." Seeing Kathy's surprise, she added, "Not you, my dear. Other people."

What other people? Kathy would have been glad to hear all about it. All about San Francisco too, as a matter of fact—who Julia had met, what she'd done—but as usual, it looked like Julia wasn't in any hurry to tell. Suddenly Kathy just didn't have the energy to pick up and put together whatever puzzle pieces Julia might consider tossing out.

"I'm surprised," Kathy said, "that you'd let them make you go to boarding school."

Julia shrugged. "If I don't like it, I'll just leave." Then she smiled slyly. "I hear that you, little one, have found true love."

Kathy flushed.

"James Holderread? How interesting."

Kathy pressed her lips together. She could play the I-have-secrets game too. "Well, it's good to see you. I'm glad you're okay." She took a couple of steps backward. "Uh, I'm going to be late for history."

"Oh, dear," Julia said. "Can't have that."

They looked at each other. It had been a long time since Kathy had worried about Julia's opinion. She just now realized how nice that had been.

"See you later." She turned and hurried away.

CHAPTER
20

KATHY LAY ON her bed, studying the ceiling. Why did this assignment seem so hard? All she had to do was come up with five hundred legible words. Write something that really happened, Mr. Dickerson had said, or make something up. It didn't matter.

She stared as if those pebbly texture bits above her were ideas and one might drop down into her blank and waiting brain. Why had she signed up for creative writing anyway?

Well, at least it gave her another class with James. He'd probably already written something completely brilliant.

James . . . Oh, no, if she started thinking about him, she'd never get anywhere on this paper . . .

The sound of voices drew her from her bed to the window. Outside, on the wet sidewalk, two little boys faced off, fists at their sides. She slid open the window.

"Hit him, Bobby!" a man was saying.

"Dad . . ."

"He started it, didn't he? Come on, stand up for yourself! Punch him back!"

Well, of all the—Kathy flew out of her room and raced to fling open the front door. Locked together now, the boys rolled in the parking strip's soggy barkdust.

"Way to go!" she shouted at the man. "How can we ever stop having wars if people like you keep telling kids to solve things by hitting each other?"

The boys scrambled to their feet. The man looked up in surprise—Mr. Sloper, Kathy saw, from two doors down.

"Kathy!" Her mother came out behind her. "What's going on?" She pulled Kathy inside.

"Did you *hear* him?" Kathy cried, jerking her arm from her mother's grasp. "Bobby didn't even want to fight and Mr. Sloper was just standing there going, 'Hit him, hit him.'"

"Was he?" Her mother frowned.

"Yes! I couldn't believe it!"

"Well, it's really not our place to—"

"Oh, right. Don't get involved. Just look the other way. Don't you see that's why everything's so screwed up? Apathy! Nobody cares about anything."

"I care, Kathy. For heaven's sakes, calm down."

"I'm going back out there." Kathy opened the door to a glimpse of Mr. Sloper steering his son away.

"Oh no you don't." Mom shut the door and blocked it, facing Kathy. "Now, I'm not saying I approve of Ted Sloper encouraging fistfights. I'm just saying I don't want my daughter standing on the front porch shouting like a banshee."

"Of course. So embarrassing. I mean, what will people *think*?"

"You're not being fair," her mother said. "We've never tried to stop you from expressing yourself."

114

"*Mo-om.*"

"Haven't I encouraged you when you've written letters to the editor? Even when I knew half the time I'd get some snide remark about it at bridge club?"

"What snide remarks?"

"Never mind. The point is, letters are better than screaming."

Kathy stalked off to her room. A letter to the editor would come a little late on this one. And it was just plain wrong to ignore injustices. Didn't somebody famous write something about evil triumphing when good men kept silent? Speaking up took such a toll on her, though. She hated the stomach-churning, adrenaline rush of a confrontation.

Now her father was in the other room getting the whole story. Great. She could hear him defending Ted Sloper, saying he'd done the right thing, trying to teach his boy never to give an inch.

She went to the window. Bits of barkdust on the sidewalk were the only signs that the calm of this gray Sunday afternoon had been disturbed. When her heart finally stopped pounding, she fell back on the bed.

She looked at the ceiling again. Geez. Now, where was she? Oh, right, an idea for a paper . . . She lay there for a moment, then bolted upright.

Duh! She would write about the fight. Something that really happened. So easy. All she had to do was put down what Mr. Sloper said, what she said, how her mother yanked her in . . .

But she should have said something about Vietnam specifically when she dashed out, just to make it all more relevant. Was it okay to change it like that? Maybe she could say it was made up. Fiction. Anyway, Mr. Dickerson sometimes wore a peace button; he'd appreciate the Vietnam bit. And wouldn't it be better if, instead of simply looking surprised, Mr. Sloper had called her a dirty hippie? No, a dirty commie peacenik hippie . . .

Oh, this was going to be good! Why not make the whole fight worse—instead of barkdust on the sidewalk afterward, blood.

She scribbled away, her pen hardly able to keep up with her brain. Wait till James reads this. She was almost glad the whole thing had happened now. Ha! Mr. Sloper never dreamed he was helping her out with her homework, never knew he was in her head, saying all sorts of obnoxious things . . .

"Kathy! Dinner's ready!"

Dinner? Already?

"Just a minute." She flipped through the pages. Twelve! Way more than she needed, but who cared? Now she just wanted to get the story right. A little bit more to go, the part where Bobby grows up and he's in jail because he's a violent criminal and his father comes to visit . . .

"Oh son," Mr. Sloper might say, "where did we go wrong?"

No, no. She scratched it out. A pitiful cliché. Been said a million times already. She needed something fresher and more subtle. Something haunting.

"Son, do you remember that mysterious long-haired girl who lived down the street? I've never forgiven myself for what I said to her . . ."

CHAPTER
21

EACH DAY DURING February's false spring, Diane—either distraught or radiant—would hunt Kathy down at school and launch into a new chapter in the drama of Steve and Diane. They were always breaking up, making up, or freaking out.

And Diane wasn't the only one going off the deep end.

David scribbled reams of torturous poetry on his favorite subject, Julia, and laughed when he got busted for marijuana.

Ted, the quiet boy who worked on the stage sets, stopped bathing and took to standing in the corner of the auditorium, facing the wall. Mr. Corwin was always having to coax him away.

It wasn't just kids either. One of the English teachers upped and quit—said he was moving to a place called Rising Star Farm, out in the Coast Range. Winnie's parents shocked her with plans for divorce. And James confided to Kathy that he'd been down in his backyard late at night when he saw the neighbor lady come stumbling off her back patio with nothing but a robe clutched around her, crying and acting drunk. And she was Janet Eddy's mother! Amazing to realize that grown-ups had these . . . *lives* going on, hassles that might not have anything to do with their kids.

Beyond the safe confines of Chintimini, police battled crowds in the Haight-Ashbury district of San Francisco and took on protesters in a segregated bowling alley in South Carolina. At a White House reception, Eartha Kitt told the president's wife in no uncertain terms she thought the war was one big mistake.

Names like Khe Sanh and Hue were intoned over the endless black-and-white film clips on TV. The draft was upped. Walter Cronkite came back from a visit to Vietnam and devoted an entire broadcast to the whole ugly mess, ending with a plea for the United States' withdrawal.

Watching this, Kathy's father was appalled. "He's not supposed to do that. He's supposed to just tell the news. State the facts."

"But Daddy," Kathy said, "it's not like the news is always just the facts."

"Sure it is. What else would it be?"

"Well, it's facts, but it's *certain* facts. The facts the government wants us to hear, put together in a way that makes us believe what the government wants us to believe."

"Here we go again," Kenny said, pushing up from the sofa, leaving the room.

"James says it goes way back to the whole Gulf of Tonkin thing," Kathy said, "and it just shows—"

"James says!" Her father gripped the arms of his chair. "Oh, then of course it's true."

"Now, honey," Mom cautioned.

"Well, excuse me, but I do get tired of having this seventeen-year-old kid held up as the big authority on everything."

"I never said he was," Kathy said, although, to be honest, she felt James knew more about the war than her father. He was the one studying it, and just because someone happened to be born earlier didn't necessarily make them smarter, right? Especially in a world where everything changed so fast.

"He's the reason you spout all this antigovernment talk, isn't he?" her father said. "For crying out loud—people running wild in the streets, these . . . hoodlums . . . burning the flag. Do you understand how that makes a guy who served his country feel? They're tearing this nation apart."

"But that's exactly what I mean about choosing facts," Kathy said. "The TV shows pictures of somebody burning a flag, you get the idea that's what everybody's doing. Maybe they don't show the kids who are just out there protesting because they think the war's wrong and somebody ought to speak up against it. And that's really what this country is supposed to be about, right? Being able to speak up?"

"But look at the message the protests send to the boys already over there," her father said. "We owe them our support."

"We owe it to them to end it," Kathy shot back. "We owe it to them to stop sending any more."

Her father's chin puckered. " 'My country, right or wrong.' That's what we were taught to believe. You think that's old-fashioned."

Kathy and her mother looked at each other. When the argument reached this point, Dad looking so beaten down, it was time to quit.

"How do you and Daddy stand it?" Kathy asked her mother when her father had gone out on the deck to smoke. "You against it and him for it?"

"Oh, Kathy, your father's not *for* the war. He's . . . baffled by the whole thing. Like being in the middle of a game and the rules are changed on you. He did what he thought he was supposed to during World War Two, and now here's his daughter, disdainful of that."

"I'm not! I know it was different. *He's* the one who can't see that Vietnam's not like World War Two. I wish it was. We could all be patriotic, pull together, and all that."

Mom nodded. "Once he's upset about something, it's true he's not too good at seeing the other side. And the protesters—well, they scare me too. People screaming about revolution. Are we going to have war right here in our own streets?"

Kathy turned off the TV and followed her mother to help clean up the kitchen. "You know, I can hardly remember when there *wasn't* the war in Vietnam."

"Maybe we should unplug the TV."

"Mom! Like that's going to unplug the war?"

"Well, sometimes I wonder—where did we get the idea we had to let it come flooding right into our house every night?"

Kathy started clearing the table. "Sometimes I think it'll go on forever."

"I know, but World War Two seemed that way too." Mom opened the dishwasher. "We'd listen to the news reports, how our troops had finally managed to capture some little island. I remember the day I looked at the map and realized there were *thousands* of those islands out in the Pacific. At the rate we were going, we'd never get them all."

Kathy already knew the rest of the story. They'd dropped the bomb on Hiroshima and Nagasaki, and that ended the war. Ended it as her father's ship plowed the Pacific toward a landing at Sasebo, Japan. Without the bomb, he always said, he and a lot of others might very likely have been killed. Without the bomb, quite a number of Kathy's generation would not have been born.

Like they actually *owed* something to that horror? God, what a thought.

And a worse one—what if somebody decided to try to end *this* war with a nuclear bomb?

"I just keep hoping," Mom said, and not for the first time, "that it'll be over before Kenny . . ."

Kathy nodded, and his name hung in the air between them, all the frightening possibilities rising. Kathy's stomach always turned over like a sick thing at the mental picture of her brother marching up into the belly of one of those troop planes bound for Vietnam.

Oh, Kenny. If something bad happened in James's life, at least he'd be ready for it. Expecting it, even. He wanted life to be about challenges and fighting to change things.

But Kenny—he seemed so innocent. Something bad happening to him would leave him totally bewildered, like Dad, like the rules had changed.

And much as Kathy resented how easy it all seemed to be for Kenny, she just couldn't stand the thought of him ever having it any other way.

"HEY, THIS IS one pep skit you won't want to miss," Kenny was telling her over dinner a few days later. "Jill's the one who cooked it all up."

"Naturally." Kathy had already heard more than enough about the cleverness of this new girlfriend of his.

"See, the rally squad's going to dress up as hippies. You know, beads and long wigs, and they'll carry peace signs and—"

"Kenny," Kathy said, "the war is not a joke."

"Who said it was?"

"Well, when you make fun of people speaking up against it . . ."

"Okay, forget it. I should have known you'd get all uptight."

When Kathy told James about the skit, he said, "I think it's time that we all, for once, put in an appearance at a pep rally."

"James? Now, what are you thinking?"

"Hey, we can't let them get away with this."

Following him into the auditorium last period that Friday, Kathy was wishing she hadn't mentioned the skit to James. Sometimes his "scenes" made her nervous.

They staked out an area in the front corner. James and all his supporters. Look at him, sitting there poised for action. The two of them were so different, she thought. He loved a confrontation, lived for it, whereas she only spoke up when she felt she absolutely had to, and then paid for it with a churning stomach. Nice girls don't argue. Would she ever get over believing that?

On the other side of the auditorium she spotted Diane, sitting with Steve and the other jocks. She was wearing one of the little jumpsuits marking her as a drill team member. Diane saw her and cocked her head questioningly. Kathy hadn't been to a pep rally since that first one their sophomore year. In response Kathy shrugged, rolled her eyes toward James. Now Steve saw Kathy too, and his eyes narrowed suspiciously. He elbowed Gary Fry and another guy. Kathy could just imagine what they were all mumbling. What are *those* people doing here?

Finally, skit time. The rally girls pranced onto the stage in fringy skirts showing plenty of thigh, their scarves tied Indian-headband style, peace symbols lipsticked on their cheeks. Overhead they brandished Flower Power signs.

James sprang up.

"The war is not a joke!"

Silence. Bewildered, the rally girls lowered their signs.

"The war is not a joke!" James turned to Kathy and the others.

"Shut up," somebody in a letterman's jacket yelled. Gary Fry.

James's group stood and took up the chant. "The war is not a joke! The war is not a joke!"

"Get him out of here!" the jocks started hollering as the entire auditorium erupted. "Shut him up!"

The vice principal grabbed James, ushering him out.

"Walkout!" James yelled as he was dragged away. His group followed, to a chorus of booing. But other kids joined the march.

"The war is not a joke! The war is not a joke!"

Outside, as soon as he was unhanded, James hopped up on a patio bench.

"People are *dying* over there right this minute," he yelled. "Babies are being killed. Do we want our school to be a place where we *laugh* at this?"

The vice principal and a couple of teachers watched

for a moment, then went inside. It was last period. Why fight it?

"Do we want to be a bunch of dumb little kids who shut their eyes to what's happening?" James went on.

People drew toward him. They were nodding, murmuring agreement, then joining his chants, punching their fists in the air. David got his guitar and started the singing; someone produced a box of colored chalk. The patio was soon covered with peace symbols and rainbows. People kept drifting out from the pep rally, swelling the crowd that milled around enjoying the rare sunshine and the heady feeling of being young and angry over a righteous cause.

Kathy saw Kenny come out to check the scene. She met his eyes calmly, then looked away, lifting her chin. She suspected they would be having a huge argument about all this at the dinner table tonight.

Watching James, she didn't care. He was worth it.

CHAPTER
22

"MORNING." KATHY THREW her books in the backseat of James's VW Bug, jumped in, and kissed him. "So what's the surprise? And why do we have to go at the crack of dawn?"

He smiled. "You'll see."

The indigo sky lightened as they drove to the nearby outskirts of town. Under her crocheted poncho, Kathy wrapped her arms around herself against the chill. The VW's heater was not the greatest.

"Your parents give you any trouble?" James said.

"Not really. Like you predicted—they don't want me out late, but what could they say about early?"

At the foot of a grassy hill, James pulled the car off the road and braked in the gravel. "Okay. Now we've got to hike up a ways." He looked doubtfully at her long skirt. "I should have told you to wear jeans."

"It's okay. I've always wanted to trail around a dewy meadow in a long dress."

James glanced at his watch, at the glowing horizon. "I think I've got this timed right."

They started up the narrow path where birds, awakening, twittered in the early chill. Stopping, Kathy looked back down on the treetops of town.

"Hurry," James said, pulling her by the hand as the sun began to rim over the blue Cascades. "We're almost there. Now, shut your eyes. Don't open them until I say so." He led her along, the pungent smell of damp earth rising around them as they parted the tender new shoots of grass. "Okay, here." He stood close behind her, hands over her eyes.

"Now?" she said, even though she was enjoying the feel of his palms resting across her cheekbones.

"Just a minute."

Finally his hands fell away.

"Oh, James!" Before her spread a field of daffodils, backlit golden by the sun's rising rays. "What *is* this?"

"Uh—a field of daffodils?"

"But how did it get here?"

"I've heard it was an old homestead."

"Oh, it's so . . . I can't believe it's been here all this time and I never knew about it."

She leaned back into his arms. Ever since James, it seemed life had become, at every turn, magically beautiful. Golden daffodils, purple mountains. And down below, in the town, the first cars on the streets. She could hear their faint hum, everyone setting off for a brand-new day. All those cars and houses, all those people inside them. Could anyone be as thrilled at being awake and alive this morning as she was?

She turned back to the field, wanting to memorize it. "Wouldn't it be great to live in a place like this? I mean like a homestead in the country?"

"Yeah, but don't actresses have to live in New York or L.A.?"

"I just mean when I look at this, I can imagine wanting my own little house. Because it wouldn't be anything like my parents' house, see. I'd have a wonderful garden and it would be a great place for kids to run around."

"You don't want kids, remember?"

"I never said that."

"You don't want to be a housewife. You don't want to be driving people around in a station wagon."

"Oh, but if I had a baby, it would be different. I'd name her Skye or Meadow or Moon—"

"Daffodil," he said rhapsodically. "Daffy for short."

"James!"

"Oh, sorry. Dilly, then?"

"Will you stop?"

"Okay, okay, but don't go for a hippie name. I'll bet everyone's going to do that."

"Okay, then, just a regular, pretty name that no one ever uses anymore. Jennifer."

"That's not bad."

"Anyway, we'd live where she could grow up close to nature, and she wouldn't have all these stupid middle-class hang-ups. I'd weave her clothes on a loom myself—"

"With wool from sheep you raised yourself!"

She turned and put her fists on her hips. "Are you laughing at me?"

"I'm not," he pleaded, but his straight face wouldn't hold. "Well, okay, I am, but I like your dream. Really."

"You do?"

"Yeah. You'd look cute churning butter too. And could I ride a horse? That is, if I could be in your dream?"

127

"You want to ride horses?"

"Sure, why not? Part of me hasn't quite gotten over the cowboy thing. So I come galloping up, right? I jump off and tell you to brush her down. Meanwhile I stomp into the house. My boots are muddy so you get mad. The kids all come tumbling out—"

"Wait, there's only one."

"Oh, no, there's more. And they're screaming with being cooped up because there's no station wagon to take them anywhere."

"James!" But she was laughing as she hauled back to pop him one.

"Aaah! Don't hit! I'm a pacifist!"

He caught her wrists and spun her into a hug from behind, her arms crossed in front of her.

"You know what my mother told me?" she said, grinning back at him over her shoulder. "She said try to find a guy who can make you laugh."

"Oh yeah?"

"Yeah." Actually her mother said "marry," not just "find." But that word was bound to scare James. Too many marriages were ending in divorce these days. Everyone was saying love should be free, like a bird. Not something to tie people down.

He turned her around and they kissed.

Oh, she could kiss him all day and never get tired of it. Before, with Gary, kissing had been such a disappointment. Maybe she'd watched too many romantic movies, arriving at the moment of her first kiss expecting it to be otherworldly somehow, like falling face first into a pile of rose petals or eating your fill of the finest chocolate. Instead it was so . . . human. Instead of celestial harp music, it was the taste of someone else's mouth.

128

But James's mouth was *better* than harp music.

"Too bad the grass is so wet," she murmured when they drew apart, thinking how much she'd like to sink down into it with him.

"We'll come back when it isn't," he answered, obviously thinking the same thing.

They kissed some more and then James said, "Well, I guess if I was really smooth I'd have brought a little wicker basket with a picturesque breakfast, huh? But this is it." From his jacket pocket he produced a crumpled cellophane package.

"Powdered doughnuts," Kathy marveled. "How'd you know those are my favorite?"

And no food before or since ever tasted so good.

CHAPTER
23

"DID YOU HEAR about New Hampshire?" James said the instant Kathy picked up the phone.

"No, what?"

"McCarthy won!"

"He did?"

"Well, forty-two percent of the vote. Wow, everybody's freaking out!" James did five minutes on how this showed there really was room for a peace platform candidate, and how he couldn't wait to sign up for the local campaign.

"Oh, by the way," he said when he finally wound down, "what did Mr. Dickerson want to see you about?"

"When?"

"After creative writing?"

"Oh, yeah. Well, he just wanted to talk to me about that little book I did. The children's story with the illustrations? He said I ought to send it in somewhere and try to get it published."

"Published? No kidding."

"Yeah. I just kind of went, uh, what for?"

"You're not going to do it?"

"Well, I doubt it. Why would I? I got the A. A plus actually—that's good enough for me. Hey, are you sure you don't want to be in *The Miser*? Tryouts start tomorrow."

A pause over the line.

"James? You still there?"

"Yeah."

"Well? Think you might try out after all?"

"I told you, Kathy. Farce isn't my thing. Farce is people acting silly."

She laughed. "Like you never act silly! Actually, you're the silliest serious person I know!"

Silence.

"And you'd be so good. It would be fun—you know—doing it together."

"No, I'm going to be busy with the campaign."

"Oh. Well, okay." He sounded so cold. He could at least acknowledge they'd miss being together. When she tried to talk about how nervous she was and how much she wanted the part of Marianne, he cut her off.

"You'll get the part," he said. "You always win."

"James." She laughed uneasily. "You know that's not true."

"You'll get it," he said.

TRYOUTS PREOCCUPIED KATHY for the next few days, and when James changed his mind about going out Saturday, she didn't think twice about his excuse of too much homework—she had tons herself.

But on Monday morning before school, when she

ran across the patio with the news that she'd been cast as Marianne, he just said, "Told you." Then he added, "Congratulations."

"James, is something wrong?"

"No."

"Come on. You've been acting really strange."

"What do you mean?"

"Well, this ought to be a happy day for me and I feel like you're . . . sort of wrecking it, frankly."

"Oh, like you've never put a damper on any day of mine."

"What? When have I ever not been happy for you when something good happened?"

He looked at her. "You really don't know, do you?"

"No, I don't."

"Huh. I thought you were smart enough to figure it out."

"Well, I guess not, so why don't you go ahead and tell me?"

He gave her a dark look. "Remember when you told me Dickerson thought you could get published?"

"Yeah."

"Well, I'd just gotten a short story back marked up so bad the paper looked diseased. And I got a C!"

She waited. "Well?"

"Well, *what?*"

"Well, how is that a case of me not being happy for you when I should have?"

"Huh? I thought we were talking about putting a damper on somebody's day."

"And you're saying I did?"

"Yeah. Completely."

"Like I should have been sympathizing or something?"

132

"Well, yeah."

"But you never told me. How'm I supposed to be sympathetic over something I don't even know about?"

"Okay, maybe you can't, but still, don't expect me to enjoy listening to you." Now he mimicked her. "Oh yes, people say I should be published but who cares?"

"You're jealous," she said, stunned. "Oh, James, please don't be like this. You're the first guy I've ever met who didn't mind seeing girls win. I always felt like you'd be just as glad for me when something good happened as I would for you."

"Well, I am," he said. "Usually. It's just that . . . I've always thought of writing as *my* territory. And you knew that."

"So it's your territory. Okay. Hey, this was a dumb little children's story."

"Doesn't matter what it was. The point is, somebody thought you could publish it."

"But I don't even care about—"

"So *what?* Don't you get it? Whether you care isn't the point. Actually that makes it worse. You should understand that—all your stories about Diane and how she never cared about playing Helen Keller as much as you would've."

"You think that shouldn't have bothered me?"

"No, I'm saying I understand why it did. So why can't you understand that you not caring about writing doesn't make me feel any better?"

"Oh, James, I'm sorry. Really. You're right."

His expression softened. *You're right.* Were those the magic words?

"Well, forget it," he said. "It's not your fault you're a good writer."

133

"Oh, come on, you're much better than I am."

His face softened another degree. She started telling him how fine his stories were—far superior to anything she'd ever written. She mentioned all the different pieces of his she'd admired and specifically why until the bell for the first class buzzed.

His smile was such a relief, such a reward, she made up her mind to keep quiet about any praise she might receive on papers in the future. Because, okay, even if this did remind her of stifling herself for Gary, it wasn't as if writing really mattered.

But later, at her locker, she stopped to think. They never *had* gotten around to talking about how neat it was that she'd been cast as Marianne. And wasn't it just amazing, how easily the word *sorry* had popped out of her mouth? All he had to do was accuse her and suddenly she was sorry all over the place. And what for? Was she supposed to be sorry he got a C? Sorry the teacher didn't recognize his brilliance? Sorry the teacher had liked her story? Were guys all like this, then? Even James? You had to tiptoe, be humble, remember to flatter?

Maybe there *was* a place for James in that stupid book. *A boy likes a girl who's clever, but not too clever, and definitely less clever than he in whatever field he's staked out for himself.*

She flipped her locker shut with a satisfying crash.

CHAPTER
24

EVERY MORNING, in the half hour before classes began, James and Kathy walked around the neighborhood of cottages next to the school. When the sun shone, the colors of the world were brilliant. When it rained, it was softly, mistily romantic. The air carried the scent of spring flowers. Why, Kathy thought, would anyone think reality like this needed altering with marijuana or LSD?

"Do you have any regrets?" James asked one day.

"About what?"

"About your life, looking back so far." He said he'd determined that lots of novels dealt with regret, which started him analyzing his own.

"I regret not getting to play Helen Keller," she said.

"Doesn't count. Has to be something you consciously did or didn't do, something you had some control over. You tried for that. There's nothing to regret about your own actions."

"Oh. Then I guess not getting a cracked heart in sixth grade doesn't count either."

"Cracked heart?"

"Didn't they have those at your grade school? Charms, two halves of a heart with some engraved saying? I know, I know, totally silly, but somehow it intrigued me, the way they fit together. I didn't have a boyfriend that year, though, so . . ." She trailed off, shrugging.

James frowned. "Nope. You're right. Doesn't count."

They walked along, swinging hands. Pink and blue hyacinths were opening in patches along the buckling old sidewalks.

"Okay, here's one," she said, brightening. "A true regret. The Whiteside Theater was having a special Nelson Eddy and Jeanette MacDonald series. My mom was sure I'd love it, so she dropped Diane and me off at *Naughty Marietta*. Everybody in the audience was at least fifty. Well, the movie was just too much. Curls, ruffles on skirts out to here, everybody mincing around. You know, 'Sweetheart, sweetheart, sweetheart!' Diane and I got to giggling, and I mean we were rolling in the aisles. Literally! And those poor people. This was their thing, probably the movie they saw the night they fell in love or something, and we were just these little brats, making fun of it."

"Wow." He smirked. "Kathy, you are truly evil."

"Okay, I know it's nothing. But when I think about it—the funny part is, I don't remember them bad-vibing us. One lady even looked back and smiled."

"Maybe they were all deaf."

"James! You know, I just wish I could go back and face them and say, 'Hey, I'm sorry.' "

He shook his head indulgently. "You are so funny."

"Okay, smarty, what are *your* earth-shaking regrets? And they better be good if you think you're going to make the Great American Novel out of them."

"That's the trouble, see. I think we're too young for major regrets. We haven't had a chance to screw up big yet. That's probably why you don't see child-prodigy writers. Kiddie musicians and math whizzes knock people's socks off, but what's a ten-year-old going to write about?"

"You're right." She thought a moment. "Do you regret that little impromptu Vietnam speech you gave when you got the Boy of the Month award?"

"Are you kidding? I think Mr. Sanders nominated me for that just to see what I'd say when I got up there."

"Well, how about the get-out-of-Vietnam bumper stickers you put on your car right before you picked me up that first time?"

"No."

"Even though I *told* you my dad would get upset?"

"I've got a right to express my convictions."

"Well, look, James, maybe this is going to be your problem—you apparently have a very high regret threshold!"

He laughed. Then he said, "Well, here's something. There was a kid in my fourth-grade class—his clothes were always dirty and he smelled bad. Kids gave him a hard time, and one day they had him cornered behind the play shed. He saw me coming and there was this . . . flash in his eyes. Hope. You know, that I'd stick up for him. But I didn't. I pretended I didn't see. I just ran over and got in the kick-ball game."

"So what happened to him?"

"He got shoved around."

"Yeah, but I mean in the end. In his life."

"I don't know. He moved or something. But that has never stopped bugging me. I can still see his eyes."

Kathy nodded. "I think that qualifies." She stooped, plucked a tiny daisy from between the sidewalk cracks, and tucked it behind her ear. "Maybe it's true what I've heard people say—it's not what you do that you regret, it's what you don't do."

They walked awhile in silence, Kathy thinking, arguing with herself to keep her mouth shut. Finally she couldn't help blurting it out.

"What about regretting that you made such a stink about Mr. Dickerson suggesting my book be published?"

"Oh, Kathy. You're still on that?"

"Well, yeah. Actually, it bugs me a lot."

"Why? I said I was sorry."

"You did?" she said dryly. "I must have missed that."

"I'd like to just forget it, okay?"

"Me, too, but I don't think I can."

"Well, it was extremely . . . immature on my part, okay? Haven't you ever said something you wished you hadn't?"

"Of course. It's not just that you said it, though. It's that I'm afraid it shows how you really feel. I thought you liked me for how I really am, and—"

"I do—"

"But that made me worry you were just like the rest of them. In the end, you'll be bugged if I do well at something."

"Okay, I admit I was jealous. Is that so weird? You're competitive too. Wouldn't you be jealous if there was something you'd been bragging about doing and then I aced you without half trying?"

"I guess."

"So I don't think it's a crime, or some huge psychological problem."

"Maybe not, but if it's going to make me feel like I ought to hold back and not succeed . . . I mean, just for instance, what if I said I *did* want to be a writer?"

"Then you should be a writer."

"But—"

"I'd just have to get used to it, wouldn't I? I mean, after that happened, I thought about it a lot and I realized, Hey, buddy, if you can't handle this, you can always go look for a girlfriend you're sure won't be better than you at anything. But what would be the point of that? I mean, do I want to throw out all the stuff that made me fall for you in the first place? And anyway, I could never go for one of those simpery girls who automatically agrees with everything you say and doesn't care about a life of her own. So, then I realized, Hey, any girl I ever like is probably going to have something that could make me jealous, so I better learn how to live with it."

"So you promise to—"

"I can't promise anything except I'll try, okay? I'll try not to be a jerk."

"Oh, James, you're not a jerk. Nobody else would even be able to figure that stuff out. They'd already be out shopping for a new girlfriend."

"Yeah, well, I don't want a new girlfriend." His arm went around her, pulled her close. "I want you."

Kathy sank against him. This is it, she thought. Cut. Print. Now is as good as it gets.

If it had been a story or a movie, Kathy would think later, this could have lasted a little longer. But she'd hardly registered the wonderfulness of the moment when she and James spotted the jocks. Gary Fry, Steve Landers, others. They were hanging out on a deserted section of a side street running along the football practice field.

"Looky here," Steve said. "It's our famous con-sci-en-tious objector."

"The big-mouth pacifist."

"And his little hippie honey."

"James?" Kathy flicked her eyes sideways at a detour.

But James moved forward.

Clinging to his hand, she took a deep breath and hustled time and a half to match his stride.

As they approached the group, somebody stepped out and hurled a fistful of ripped-up lawn daisies in their faces. "Peace!"

"Hey," Kathy said, brushing the petals away from her eyes.

"Love and flowers!"

"Pacifistics don't believe in hitting back, isn't that right?"

"Try 'im, Landers. Give 'im a punch."

"James?" Kathy's voice slid up.

"Come on." He pulled her off the sidewalk into the street, skirting them.

The jocks were right behind, jostling closer.

A hand reached forward, clamped James's shoulder, and spun him around. An elbow cocked, a fist jabbed. From James's nose, an explosion of bright red blood.

It ran through James's fingers as he lifted his eyes to the one who'd hit him.

"Jesus," someone said.

Even Steve Landers, knuckles bloody, looked

startled. Everyone stared at him. He shifted his weight, glanced around for support. None came. He laughed—a sick, uncertain sound—then turned and punched James again.

James's head snapped back; Kathy's hands flew to her mouth.

James touched his nose, then squinted at Steve as if something incomprehensible had been said. "Are you finished?"

Gary Fry stepped forward. "Enough, already, Landers."

"You jerk!" Kathy threw herself at Steve. "You stupid ape!"

"Kathy, no," James said.

"You stupid idiot!" She beat her fists on his chest, the *C* of his letterman's jacket. "You are the most pathetic . . . pathetic excuse . . ."

"Hey, knock it off!"

Gary Fry wedged between them.

"Kathy, don't." James pulled her away.

They stumbled toward the school, and behind them Kathy heard mumblings—"Geez, Landers, way to go," mixed with his whining protests, "You told me to, man!"

"Oh, James," she kept saying. "Oh, James, you're bleeding all over the place."

Did this really just happen? she was thinking. You go for months, years, living inside your head, making up stories about what it might be like when life actually started, and then . . . bam! A punch in the face.

At the patio, she got him to lie down on a bench and put his head back. Friends gathered, outraged. Winnie ran in and grabbed a fistful of paper towels from the girls' room.

"Let's get 'em," somebody said. "They can't do this."

"No, don't," James said.

"Well, somebody ought to report it."

James sat up. "Forget it."

As people started drifting off to class, Kathy saw Diane come running out and stop, staring at James. Someone must have told her. Her eyes met Kathy's across the distance. She glanced toward the group of boys coming down the street toward the school, then whirled and ran back inside. Suddenly it struck Kathy—it was awful to see your boyfriend get bloodied, but how much worse to be the girlfriend of a loser who would do such a thing.

James went in to clean up, and Kathy was left pacing. She kept running the whole episode over in her mind, exactly what each person had said and done, and what she'd felt as each frame of this mental film had clicked by. It had gone so shockingly fast, and yet in a strange way, time had slowed down.

I am one lousy excuse for a pacifist, she thought. I could have scratched Steve Landers's eyes out.

But maybe there *was* something to nonviolence. Look how James's refusal to fight back had stopped Steve, stopped all of them. When they saw the blood.

Oh, James. God, she loved him. She more than loved him, she *admired* him. It all reminded her of *To Kill a Mockingbird* and the way Atticus just wiped off his glasses when the bigots spit on him.

Now the jocks reached the patio, shoving each other, joking self-consciously.

Kathy crossed her arms over her chest, for the first time noticing the blood on the sleeve of her favorite smock dress. She glared as they walked by, pretending they didn't see her. Gary made eye contact, a flickering sort of apology, and another guy gave her a goofy grin and flashed the peace sign.

Then she felt an arm over her shoulder. Kenny.

"I just heard," he said.

"Oh, Kenny."

"That guy is such a jerk."

She nodded, and they stood there in one of those perfectly silent moments where nothing is said and everything is said.

"You okay?" Kenny said to James when he came back out.

James nodded, shrugging.

Then the three of them went back into the building together.

CHAPTER
25

"HE'S ACTUALLY A sweet guy, down deep," Diane told Kathy, apologizing for Steve the third or fourth time. "Sometimes he just gets . . . you know."

Kathy nodded, wishing Diane would quit already. How many more times could Kathy sit still for this before she blurted out her true feelings: that Steve was bad news and Diane ought to dump him? As if Diane would ever listen.

"You didn't punch James," Kathy said instead. "Steve did."

"I know, but I feel . . . responsible."

"Well, don't. Nobody's blaming you, okay?"

James seemed to be the first one to forget the whole thing, and while the whole school was still talking about the incident from one corridor to the next, he was already on to a new scheme of running for class president.

"But James," Kathy said, "you've always called student council and all that a stupid, juvenile waste of time."

"It is," he said cheerfully. "But it's not like I'm

going to win. I'll just do the campaign. Bully pulpit, right? The other guys will talk about their great experiences qualifying them for this—Youth Legislature, Boys' State. I, meanwhile, will talk about the resistance!"

"What if you accidentally get elected?"

"Well, then I'll *really* get everyone whipped up about the war."

"You think the administration'll let you get away with that?"

"Let 'em try to stop me. It's still a free country. We've still got free speech. And anyway, people are ripe for it—teachers, everybody. Ever since the Tet Offensive—geez, even President Johnson's own advisers are starting to admit they don't know what the hell we're doing over there. This might turn out to be the beginning of the end. I mean, what can our government say when everyone's sons start coming home in body bags? And anyway, even if I never mentioned the war, there's a million issues that ought to be brought up. Dress code stuff. This business of wanting to close the campus. Parents trying to ban *One Flew Over the Cuckoo's Nest.* And locker searches. I don't know why somebody hasn't taken them to court on that."

Kathy couldn't get over James's energy, his grasp of politics and the wider world. Whatever he did— debate team, writing songs or articles for the paper, running for office—it was all about getting up and saying what needed to be said. Even being in *The Crucible* was, for him, more about its theme than about acting.

But Kathy was not nearly so interested in the theme of a play as in whether she had lots of good, dramatic scenes and wonderful costumes. For her, the spring play meant a gown with a sweeping train that took hours of practice to accommodate, and her long hair curled with rags into bouncy corkscrew curls.

"It's fun," she told James. "Who cares if the play has some big heavy moral?"

My God, she thought. Listen to me. I sound like my mother.

Well, so what? She was an actress! Finally, she'd found her true calling.

But was it already too late?

"Have you heard about this new *Romeo and Juliet* movie Zeffirelli's doing?" she asked James. "They've got this girl for Juliet—Olivia somebody. I can't stand it! People my age already doing movies and stage plays, and here I am, stuck in this dumb town. I ought to be in New York right this minute!"

Mr. Corwin started calling her Marjorie Morningstar. When she learned this was the title character in a novel by Herman Wouk, she immediately got it from the library. How she wept when she reached the end and found that budding actress Marjorie Morningstar ended up a run-of-the mill housewife with four children.

A housewife! Why was the world so full of all these grown-ups who smiled at young, brave talk of wonderful careers and relished assuring you that your transformation into a dreary, middle-class mom was all but inevitable?

"I hate that!" she cried to James. "Why did Herman Wouk have to write that ending anyway? First she's all fired up with dreams, then he takes them away, like that's how it has to be, like no matter what you want

146

or plan or try for, it's already determined that you're going to wind up exactly like everybody else."

"Kathy." He was calm. "You won't."

"You don't think so?"

"Of course not. You could never be like everybody else."

"Oh, James, you don't know how much it means to me for you to say that." And then she added, "You could never be like everyone else either."

"I know. So don't worry about that stuff. We're going to live our lives the way *we* want. Hey, the whole world's going to be different, okay?"

Even with everything falling apart around them, this energy of his made her feel that somehow they really could make it better. Or at least it couldn't all go to hell without a lot of hollering about it first.

Sometimes, coming out after rehearsals, she'd see the nonconformist types playing soccer, and even way across the field she could tell which one was James, not just by the flash of his black hair either. Like one of the English ballads she used to sing: *One day I was lookin' o'er my father's castle wall . . . I spied all the boys a-playin' with the ball . . . My own true love was the flower of them all . . .*

And those nights after they'd met to study at the library, when they'd find some quiet place to park . . . *This* was what all the grown-ups hoped you wouldn't discover. All those health class jokes about telling boys to go take a cold shower—they talked like it was war, with clearly drawn battle lines. You against him. The losers got babies and VD. But they left out the part about love.

You could even read grown-up books and not

understand. She'd thought she was getting away with a lot, reading *Hawaii* last summer, a book in which people "screwed." Big deal! They did this, they did that. No hint of the inexpressible sweetness she and James had found.

Oh, James, who would stop the instant she said stop but never before. Such a terrifying and thrilling realization: He had no stopping place in mind at all! Well, maybe in theory, when they had one of their cool, calm discussions about it. But not when it was happening. When a stopping place counted, it was all up to her.

In the middle of it he was nothing but soft, murmured arguments. Why not touch here? Or there? What would it hurt? And of course it never hurt; far from it. Made you frantic to discover just how wonderful the next little move might be. Every encounter became a skirmish. They were playing tug-of-war and he was slowly, sweetly and oh so persuasively dragging her over the line.

Oh God, she had thought sex was way off in the future. Suddenly, this crazy spring when the entire nation was freaking out in a thousand different ways, this spring when life was better than she'd dared dream, going all the way seemed frighteningly close.

And it couldn't be. Out of the question. The issue of sin aside, Kathy could hardly fathom the horror of standing in front of her parents and saying those words: "I'm pregnant." She could just picture the shocked disappointment on their faces. Daddy might actually find himself at a loss for an appropriate cliché. She had already been allowed to overhear the warning about a guy not wanting to buy a cow if he could get the milk for free, but she couldn't imagine what on earth her father would say if the worst actually happened. And then to be shipped off to some maternity home . . . Or what if you weren't? Maybe it would be even more miserable, locked at home for months with parents spitting mad at you. And then to go through labor, knowing you'd be giving the baby up for adoption—a baby she and James had made . . . Oh, why did she have to have such a vivid imagination? She'd probably have a lot more interesting life if she weren't so good at picturing the horrible consequences of everything.

She began to think about people who were rumored to have gone all the way.

Julia, of course, was too sophisticated to have *ever* been a virgin—or so she let people imagine.

Then there was that Debbie what's-her-name, who used to wear a black bra under a white blouse. But she and a couple of others like her didn't seem to be around school anymore. Maybe they'd dropped out or gotten married or something.

There were rumors about Trish and Tom, king and queen of the senior class, who'd been going together forever and walked the halls like a bored married couple, pinkies linked.

And Sue Shraeder. People said she'd gone off last year, "to visit an aunt," but everyone knew when she came back, she'd left behind a baby put up for adoption. The student body responded by promptly voting her onto the varsity rally squad. Hey, they were way too cool to think this was some big sin, right?

"I don't know how much longer I can resist," Kathy finally confided to Diane. "Whoever guessed it could be such a hassle?"

Diane went pink to her eyebrows and didn't answer.

"I mean, how do you handle it, Diane? Do you guys end up fighting about it all the time?"

"Not anymore." And Diane simply looked at Kathy, waiting for her to get it.

Oh. Kathy stared, comprehension dawning. "Oh, Diane." Before, Diane had merely been way ahead of her. Now she stood, Kathy saw, on the far side of a huge divide.

"You'll give in pretty soon," Diane said, "when James starts saying if you won't, he'll find someone who will."

"But James would never say that."

"Oh, he might not come right out and say it, but that's what they all think."

"No! James is different. I mean, that'd be like saying one girl was the same as the next and it doesn't even matter who you . . . you know."

Diane's face flushed an even deeper shade. She got very busy stacking her books.

"Diane?"

"I gotta go."

Watching her walk away, Kathy realized they would not be talking about any of this ever again.

ONE NIGHT WHILE Kathy was baby-sitting, she noticed a packet of birth control pills on the windowsill over the kitchen sink. Wait—weren't the McKennas Catholic? Hadn't the pope said birth control was a no-no? Yet here were the pills.

Kathy leaned forward, peering at the little tablets in their plastic bubbles. The Pill. Magic. Take these and you could go all the way without ever worrying.

No fear of pregnancy, the solution to everything. Wouldn't that be heaven?

How on earth could you ever get your hands on them, though? Discussing it with old Dr. Temple was out of the question, even if he didn't tell her mother.

Oh, it was awful to be young! Everything so scary and confusing, grown-ups forever pointing out how important every decision you made would prove to be.

But it was wonderful to be young! Everything so new and exciting, thousands of choices and things constantly happening for the very first time.

KATHY AND JAMES sat in the first balcony row at the Simon and Garfunkel concert, and in the sweet strains of "Scarborough Fair," Kathy heard love and loss, and the fear of James being swept up in a distant war. It felt so good to weep until the tears ran down her face and neck, down inside her blouse. And when they sang "She once was a true love of mine," James squeezed her hand, and she looked at him and bit her lip, and tears poured out fresh. She was so happy and so sad, like she was already looking back on this, like the two of them were part of a haunting song she would remember all her life.

CHAPTER
26

AT NINE-THIRTY MONDAY, April 8, a clear but chilly morning, Kathy stashed her books in her locker and started across the school's patio, half expecting a teacher to stop her. "Just tell them you're going to the march and that's it," James had advised her. "They've canceled morning classes at the university. Besides, what can they do?"

Right. What could they do about *anything*?

Martin Luther King, Jr., shot dead. What would be next?

She climbed into James's car with David and Winnie. They drove to the university and joined a solemn group of students, faculty members, and townspeople milling around the quad. Hundreds? A thousand?

Her parents were always warning her to avoid mob scenes. Looking around, though, Kathy didn't see this group as ready to explode. Everyone was angry, yes, but it was a sad, disgusted anger, not the rage that builds and erupts.

Marching right down the middle of the street felt

strange. She hadn't done this since . . . since . . . oh, no, what a thing to think of now. But walking along, holding James's hand, she flashed on the memory of the kiddie parade, herself as a fairy princess, holding the hand of four-year-old Petey Stevens in his Superman tights and cape. Remembering, she smiled and glanced up, then caught herself at the grave expression on James's face.

Demonstrations like this were taking place all over the country, every one of them peopled with marchers thinking thoughts far more profound and appropriate than hers. This great leader fallen, this hope for peace and justice and equality destroyed . . . This was what they'd been hearing for the last few days. Shame filled her to realize she didn't feel as grief-stricken as she should have . . . not in a personal, I-don't-want-to-get-out-of-bed-this-morning way. After all, it was terrible, it was awful, to think such a thing could happen in this country.

Only—she had James now. She couldn't *wait* to get up in the morning, couldn't wait to see his face. Even if something bad happened, she looked forward to hearing what he had to say about it.

Since James, the whole world looked different. True, things were as lousy as ever. Nothing had improved. But somehow she didn't feel so depressed about it. When she remembered the Martin Luther King march in years to come, she knew it would always be, for her, about James, the two of them, together on this day. She pictured herself walking beside him through the future, whatever happened. Married people must go through the years like this, she was thinking, their lives playing out against the backdrop of big, history-shaping events. And what would those coming events be? More assassinations? Wars? Famines? Environmental catastrophes?

With James to hold her hand, she could almost stand to think about it. And maybe that was the best you could hope for, maybe that was enough—a hand to hold.

She scuffed along in her suede boots, glancing at his sober profile as they passed the library. He knew so much more about civil rights than she did. Ever since the news last Thursday night, he'd been rehashing it all—King's "I Have a Dream" speech, the March on Selma. Kathy had listened and nodded, hoping he wouldn't notice she didn't necessarily follow everything he said, hadn't read every last book and newspaper article he assumed she had.

Her experience with Negroes was pitifully limited. She'd been raised on the belief they deserved the same treatment as anyone else, but here in Chintimini, this notion was rarely put to any sort of test. Negroes definitely *weren't* treated the same. How could they be, standing out like they did? When a Negro family moved to the nearby army base, Kathy's third-grade teacher made such a fuss over everyone being nice to the new little girl that Tommy Blake and Stu Miller got in a shoving match over who got to teeter-totter with her first, and Stu broke his arm falling to the pavement. Witnessing this couldn't count for much experience in race relations. Whenever Kathy did encounter a Negro, she tried so hard to be color-blind, she ended up a twitching study in self-consciousness.

At the county courthouse a flag snapped in the raw breeze. The crowd massed on the lawn around a lectern and listened to the president of the university speak of the terrible irony of a man so dedicated to the principles of nonviolence losing his life to violence. These are frightening, perilous times, he said, times that require the utmost effort on the part of each one of them to stamp out every form of prejudice and bigotry.

Then a Negro man stood up to the mike. "White people ought to search their souls," he said, "because anyone who preaches bigotry is as guilty as the one who pulled the trigger."

Kathy glanced at James. She had certainly never preached bigotry. She felt guilty just the same. Because she'd never ridden any freedom buses or marched in any protests either. All she'd ever done was sit around and brood over those awful white people down South who went around blowing up churches, setting vicious dogs on peaceful Negroes, and screaming at frightened little Negro girls as they walked into integrated schools for the first time.

She knew better than to call Negroes "colored." Big deal. Here in this nicey-nice town of cookie-cutter houses—what did she know about picking cotton in the hot sun or living in the ghetto? What had she ever done to help the situation? What right did she have to enjoy her life and be happy about being in love when other people were so oppressed and miserable?

Now James turned to her. Surely he'd have some sort of answer to this.

"On our way back to school," he said, "do you want to stop for a shake and fries?"

CHAPTER
27

KATHY DRAPED HERSELF over the banister and watched her mother snap pictures of Kenny in his tux.

"Mo-om!" he kept protesting, but obviously he was enjoying the fuss, the way his utter transformation had startled them all.

"Just a couple more, honey. I can't get over how grown up and handsome you look."

"Did I ever look that slick in one of those?" Dad asked.

"Of course you did," Mom said.

Kathy sniffed. "Is that Dad's Old Spice I smell?"

"Okay with you?" Kenny said.

Dad turned to Kathy. "So why aren't you dressed up? Aren't you going to the prom?"

Kathy rolled her eyes. Her father had eaten his way through at least three dinners where the entire conversation had been on the subject of the prom.

"You and James could double with Kenny and Jill," Mom had suggested one time. Kenny had a coughing fit, and Kathy said, "Forget it, Mom. I know you think that'd be real cute, but Kenny and I are *never* going to double."

Just last night Mom had served up guilt with the chocolate pudding. "I can't help envying the mothers of these girls. I always thought I'd get to sew prom dresses for you, Kathy."

"Sorry." Was this fair? Her mother got to help with her gorgeous spring play costume.

"I hate to see you miss something that ought to be one of the highlights of high school, just because—"

"It's a sosh thing, Mom."

"Oh, that's silly."

"Mo-om! It's too late now anyway."

"I bet you'll regret it. Don't you remember back in junior high, you and Diane, poring over the prom issue of *Seventeen*?"

"Please. Don't remind me. That was so stupid."

How could her father eat meatloaf and pork chops and Jell-O through all this and then wonder why she wasn't standing there now in a long dress and heels with her hair piled and sprayed in a tower on top of her head?

"So, Kathy, what *are* you doing tonight?" Kenny asked. "Because I promised Jill you guys were just kidding about that horse thing."

"Horse thing?" Mom said.

Kathy smiled. She and her friends had toyed with a plot to crash the prom as the Four Horsemen of the Apocalypse. "Plague," she murmured to Kenny. "Pestilence . . ."

"Kathy?" Kenny said.

"Oh, don't worry. James and I are going to *The Graduate*."

"Again?" Mom said.

"We like it, okay? Hey, Mom, have you noticed Jill has pierced ears?"

Her mother pretended not to hear this. "Jill's mom will take pictures, won't she?" she asked Kenny. "Because I've got to have one of the two of you together."

"There might be a photographer at the dance," Kenny said.

"Oh, wonderful. Be sure to have pictures taken, then. Don't worry about the money—we'll pay."

"So are you guys going out to dinner?" Kathy asked.

"That's the plan," Kenny said.

"What's it going to be? Taco Bell? Shakey's Pizza?"

"No, smarty, everybody's going to Lee's Chinese."

"Really?" It was hard to picture Kenny and Jill sitting in a real restaurant, ordering and paying all by themselves, acting grown up.

"What's Jill's dress like?" Mom asked. "Did she tell you the color?"

"Um, pink? No. Blue? I forget."

"You said it was blue," Kathy offered. "That's why you're wearing that sash deal."

Kenny peered down at his baby blue satin cummerbund. "Oh, yeah. Well, the important thing is, I got the right flower." He picked up his corsage box. "This gardenia thing."

"Lemme see," Kathy said.

Kenny opened the glossy white box and they bent forward to catch the fragrance.

"Don't touch it," Mom warned. "Gardenias wilt so easily."

"I'd have wanted roses," Kathy said. "And a voile

dress with princessy, banded puffed sleeves and a skirt that floats out . . ." She started to twirl, then stopped when her eyes met her mother's.

Well, people in her crowd just didn't go to the prom, that's all.

Kenny accepted the car keys from Dad, a misty-eyed kiss from Mom.

The instant the door closed behind him, Kathy recognized the gnawing feeling she had for what it was—regret.

CHAPTER
28

"KATHY?" HER MOTHER called. She was out on the back deck, reading the evening paper.

"Yeah?"

"Honey, has James said anything about . . . well, about anything?"

"Mom." Kathy stood with her face against the screen door. "What kind of a question is that?"

"Says here in the paper his father's accepted a teaching appointment in Massachusetts."

"What?" Kathy's stomach lurched. She pushed open the door. "Let's see." She scanned the brief article in the university news section. "This is—I don't know . . ."

"He never mentioned it?"

Kathy didn't answer directly. "They're probably planning to let James stay here for senior year. Yeah, because he's running for class president, you know. The speeches are this week."

"Still, wouldn't he have said something?"

"Maybe not." She tried for a casual lilt. "Not if . . .

well, you know . . . if it really doesn't have anything to do with him."

Her mother's eyebrows went up.

"Mom, you don't understand. James doesn't toe the line for his parents like I do. Some people have more backbone."

No argument. Her mother just looked at her. Suddenly Kathy couldn't stand one more instant of that expression—so full of doubt and pity.

She bolted for the phone.

"Tell me it's not true," she said when she got James on the line.

"Oh, Kathy."

Her heart sank.

"We just found out for sure ourselves," he said.

"And you're going *with* them?"

A pause. "As opposed to what?"

"But . . . but, what about us? I mean, they know about us, don't they? Know that this isn't just some silly junior-high going steady thing?"

"Yeah, they know. Actually . . . I have the feeling they think this might be best."

"*Best!* Why?"

Another pause. "You know."

Her face went hot. She *did* know. "You haven't been *telling* them anything . . . ?"

"Of course not, but they're not dumb. They were young once too. And what's going to happen here? You've said yourself you didn't know how long we could go on without . . ."

"Oh, James . . ."

"And we *are* kind of young to be so serious . . ."

She burst into tears.

"Kathy, don't."

"Well, did you argue? Did you yell and refuse?"

"Of *course*."

"Because I've never seen you go along with anything you were against without at least yelling about it."

"Kathy, you think I want to leave? But it's no use." She hung up.

"Oh, Kathy," her mother said, following her as she careened into her bedroom to fall across the bed.

"What's going on?" Kathy heard her father saying as he came up the stairs from the rec room.

"I wish I'd never met him," Kathy cried.

Mom sat on the edge of the bed. "You don't mean that, honey." She looked back at Dad, who now stood in the doorway. "It's James. He's moving."

"I do too mean it if it's going to end up like this! I wish he could just run away or something. Just . . . refuse to go." This was *James*, after all. James, who seemed so independent she hardly thought of him as having parents. He was going to let them wreck his life? Her life? If he ran away to Canada or something it would at least be dramatic and grown up. But this was pathetic, being hauled away by Mommy and Daddy. "I'm never going to love anybody ever again!"

"Oh, now, you know what they say, Kathy." Her father took a step into the room. "It's better to have loved and lost, than never to have—"

"Aaaugh!" She hurled a pillow at him.

He backed up. "What did I—?"

"Kathy, honey, he's moving," Mom said. "Not dying. Nobody says you have to break up."

"Oh, sure. You don't think putting three thousand

miles between us will pretty well break us up? That's exactly what the parents do in those old novels when they want to wreck a romance—ship the girl off to Europe!"

"Nobody's doing this to break you up."

"But they don't care. They think it's just as well. And I'll bet you're glad too. You never liked him."

"That's not true," Mom said. "How could I not like someone who cheered you up so much?"

"Well, Daddy didn't."

"I just thought he acted a little too big for his britches," Dad muttered. "That's all."

"And please don't try to tell me I'll get over it," Kathy said. "Because remember *The Miracle Worker*? 'There'll be other plays,' you said. 'You'll get over it.' But I won't, because none have meant as much as that one did right then. And I'll never get over James either. I don't want to! Because what kind of a life can you be having if everything turns into something you just get over and say, 'Oh, that was dumb. I can't believe I ever got so upset!' "

"Honey, honey . . ."

"Oh, geez." Kathy sat up straight. "I just thought of something. This is . . ." She sniffed, rubbing tears off her cheeks. "Look at us! Do you guys ever get tired of doing this scene? I lie on the bed and cry. Mom, you sit here patting me. Dad, you stand in the doorway like you're afraid of me."

Her parents looked at each other, bewildered.

"I'm not kidding! I swear, Dad, I am always going to remember you standing in the doorway."

"You'd stand back too if you knew you were bound

163

to say the wrong thing." He looked dejected. "I haven't managed to say the right thing since you were about four years old."

"Oh, Daddy."

Mom was looking at her as if from a distance. "It's interesting the way you do this. I wonder if it isn't kind of . . . unusual to be so . . . aware."

"I think it just goes to show she's not that upset," Dad said, cheerful again. "A person who's really upset can't stop and watch herself."

"That's not true!" Kathy protested.

The phone rang. Her father answered it and came back saying it was James.

"I don't want to talk to him now."

"What should I tell him?"

"Tell him I'll call him when I'm done being stupid and hysterical!" Because she could see herself all too clearly. This . . . *affliction* of watching everything from the outside never made the painful stuff any less painful; it just made her constantly aware of how ridiculous she probably looked.

They left her alone, and Kathy cried until her eyes stung, her head throbbed, and the air itself had gone dark and grainy. At some point she heard Kenny come in. What sick thing was it that made her strain to catch the murmured words explaining her absence at the table? All through dinner's distant clink of silverware she sobbed.

I must be a wreck, she thought after a solid hour of this. I'll bet I look awful. Exhausted and curious, she got up and peeked in her dresser mirror. Auuuggh! For a moment she stared at the wreckage of her face. Then she dragged herself to the open window, propped her elbows on the sill, and through the faintly dusty screen inhaled a deep breath of fragrant spring air.

The world outside looked the same. You'd never guess an earthquake had struck.

CHAPTER
29

"YOU KNEW?" KATHY cried, pushing back from James, bracing against the inside of the car door. "You knew all year your father was applying for another job?"

"I thought about telling you," James pleaded, "but I didn't want to get you upset over something that probably wasn't going to happen anyway. I mean, this isn't the first time he's sent out applications."

She stared out the car's open window. "I don't believe this."

"Look, would I have bothered to write speeches for the student body campaign if I really thought I was leaving?"

Grudgingly, she let him pull her back. "I guess not."

"Besides, I couldn't stand to think it might happen myself."

She sagged against him. It wasn't like he'd said he didn't love her anymore. That would be worse. And it wasn't like he was dead. It wasn't *that* final.

It just felt like it.

Kathy's life became nothing but a wander through a fog called *James is leaving.*

Music became her enemy. She wanted to ban all radios. "Where Have All the Flowers Gone?" left her weepy; "Scarborough Fair" was an emotional ambush.

Certain smells were like traps too. Once James left a flannel shirt in her locker, and when she opened it, releasing his cozy, familiar smell, her throat closed so tight it ached.

She dragged around, conscious of her parents' concern. "This too shall pass," her dad said, trying not to look overly relieved to be heading out the door, escaping to the school's annual sports banquet with Kenny.

This too shall pass.

She didn't believe it for a minute.

"Can't you at least have fun together until he goes?" her mother would plead.

Fun? Sure.

Of course she remembered life before James—she just couldn't remember what had made it worth living. And was it only last week she hadn't known he'd have to go? Life was perfect then, and she hadn't even appreciated it. What had she been worried about? The stupid prom? An exam?

They went to the movie *2001: A Space Odyssey*, which gave Kathy a case of the deep, dark, existential creeps. The music—that tortured souls' choir—and the nightmarish image of death as a coldly elegant hotel room . . . She couldn't stand the film's vision of the future—sterile, impersonal, cold. Was it going to be like that? She wanted her feet on earth, actual dirt, with the warmth of the sun, the sheltering shade of trees, and the smell of flowers—everything that was rich and alive and made a person feel anchored. She wanted people, not computers.

Who but James would understand? Now that he was leaving, who would hold her and let her cry, tell her she *wasn't* alone and wasn't psychotic just because she was freaking out over a movie everyone else said was so cool?

Her own future looked completely empty. When James left, she'd be as lost as that astronaut floating untethered into the void. All the stories she'd made up about what might happen next year were wiped off the slate. Just like it said in some old song, she'd built her world around somebody. Now look what had happened.

Would it have been easier to take if he'd gone around looking as miserable as she felt? It bothered her to see him goofing off on the soccer field, or sitting in the cafeteria discussing the presidential elections as if normal life were continuing, as if Lyndon Johnson deciding not to run for reelection and Robert Kennedy declaring mattered one little bit compared to the fact that pretty soon, Kathy and James would have to say goodbye, maybe forever. Once James talked almost enthusiastically about some underground paper in Boston he might write for next year.

Was it possible she didn't mean as much to him as he did to her?

"Boys don't always show their feelings," her mother said.

"And anyway," her father added, "there's lots of other fish in the sea."

"Oh, Daddy," she said. "Not for me."

"Phooey, you'll have all kinds of guys in love with you in college."

"I don't think so."

"Honey!" Mom said. "It breaks my heart to hear you talk like that. How did you ever get such a low opinion of yourself?"

"I don't. I think I'm fine. But look around. There aren't a lot of guys who like girls like me."

Her parents traded a look. They knew this was true.

"That's only because they're immature right now," Mom said. "It'll be different later. You'll see."

"Well, I'm sorry, but I don't think there'll ever be anybody like James."

"Now, now . . ."

"Do you realize," Kathy said, "that he is probably the only person in my life who has never once said to me, 'Gee, you're no fun'?"

THE DAYS PASSED, and Kathy kept on writing her papers and studying for finals. Pathetic. Here her life was practically ending, and she didn't have the guts to rebel, chuck out her schoolwork, and just give herself over to grief.

Now that she had a good reason, she went down and passed the test for her driver's license. James's parents were going ahead to Massachusetts. He'd be allowed to stay with another family, finish the year, and take the train back East. A person who hoped for the honor of driving him to the station for a private farewell would have to be a person with a license.

Gradually she began to invent new stories of the future, stories to make the best of this. If life had to be sad, at least it could be beautifully sad.

She pictured herself on a cold, rainy day next winter, pulled close to the fire, penning lines of love and longing to James on blue, rosebud-sprinkled paper. (She had often admired this stationery downtown—now she'd have an excuse to buy some.) She'd write stories about what was going on in her life, and every envelope would be a work of art, bearing sealing wax or detailed drawings, or a small, special picture cut from a magazine, the significance of which only he would comprehend. She saw him standing in the snow at his mailbox (It snowed back there, right?), holding in his gloved hand an envelope on which was pasted the tiny picture of a daffodil. It would be like holding spring again, as he recalled that dew-spangled morning in the daffodil field . . .

James would become a legend at school, and when fond stories were told about the rebellions he'd led, the stands he'd taken, heads would turn toward her in recognition of her status as his beloved. It would be she who would open the mailbox at the curb and find his letters, she who would keep them tied in a ribbon, those sheets of notebook paper covered with his words.

He wasn't even gone yet and she was already looking forward to them—his words.

CHAPTER
30

"ALL RIGHT, ALL right," her mother said. "You win. Get your ears pierced."

"Mom. You mean it?"

"If that's what you want. I'm tired of fighting this."

"But—"

"Don't tell me you're going to argue the other side now."

"No! I just—well, what made you change your mind? Is it 'cause you're feeling sorry for me about James?"

"No. Well, actually, yes, but mainly it just doesn't seem worth trying to hold the line anymore."

"Oh. Gee. I wonder what Dad'll say. And Kenny."

"Just keep your hair over your ears at the dinner table and they'll never notice."

"Really?"

"Really. Sometimes I've felt I could put a ring through my nose and it'd go right past those two."

Kathy touched one earlobe. "Suppose it'll hurt much?"

Her mother smiled sweetly. "Like torture."

"Mom!"

"Now I see how I should have handled this. If I'd *insisted* you get your ears pierced, you would have fought me off for years."

THROUGH THE YELLOW pages, Kathy found a woman doctor whose rate would be just ten dollars, probably not nearly as much, she thought with satisfaction, as her mother hoped she'd have to fork over. Because those were Mom's conditions—a doctor to do it and Kathy had to pay.

On the appointed afternoon, she sat in the waiting room of the doctor's storefront office with half a dozen worn-out women and three times as many children. The limp kids sprawled across their mothers' laps, and the hyper ones bounced—coughing, fussing, whining.

Kathy fingered the card punched with a set of small gold button earrings she'd purchased. She felt unforgivably young, healthy, and slender. My God, look what having babies did to a person. Not fair, of course. No one could look her best after being up all night with sick kids. But one girl wasn't much older than Kathy herself, and she already had two kids. Wasn't she that Carla somebody who'd been in ninth grade when Kathy was in seventh?

Kathy opened her yearbook, releasing the sharp smell of newly printed paper. The books had been distributed final period today, and she hadn't had time to study hers yet.

Besides her official class picture, the other shots of her were all from the plays. James, though, was everywhere—behind a podium, on the soccer field. Somebody even thought he looked picturesque sprawled on a stairwell window seat, reading Dostoyevsky.

Thinking of him, Kathy glanced at her watch. He was excited about the California primary today. He'd be following the news coverage. No one really imagined McCarthy could win, he said, but then, no one had thought he'd win in New Hampshire. And who'd have thought he'd be the first to beat a Kennedy when he won here in Oregon?

She continued flipping through the yearbook. Oh, no—Julia, solemnly posed beside Kenny's girlfriend in the dance decoration committee shot taken back in September. How'd she get in there? Julia wouldn't loop crepe paper around a gym if her life depended on it!

A shot of Diane and Steve at the Winter Formal— Diane smiling at the camera, Steve keeping an eye on her. Something in his expression . . . Oh, Diane, she thought. Get away. You deserve better.

David and Winnie at a set construction party last fall. Funny how everyone already looked slightly different than they had back then, like they were all growing up and changing in time-lapse photography or something.

She almost missed the picture of her brother. Not the one where he was horsing around in the pool with his pals. That one jumped right out at you. But this other one—Kenny looking thoughtful, sitting by himself on the football field bleachers . . .

Pages turning, this bittersweet sense of time passing. Kathy felt relieved to close the book when the nurse finally called her name and led her to an examination room.

After another wait, Dr. Madsden appeared, a sturdy older woman with close-cropped gray hair.

"So," she said, "I suppose you want the Pill. Let's get a pelvic."

"No!" Kathy flushed. "I mean, that's not—" Did it show, then, how much she thought about it? Were lots of girls her age coming in for it? Would it really have been that easy to get a prescription?

"Oh," the doctor said, checking the clipboard. "I see. Ears pierced."

Kathy nodded, exhaling, trying to get her breath. Even if the Pill worked the first day you took it—which she understood was not the case—it was still too late, with James leaving, to get going on all this now. Sex seemed, once again, like something for the future. And that felt okay. She could stay a safe distance from the world of those women in the waiting room. It was good to be seventeen, she thought, to be sitting on the end of this examination table only for the purpose of getting her ears pierced. It was wonderful to be able to take a pass, for now at least, on the hassle of pulling off her jeans and submitting to a pelvic exam.

"I feel kind of silly," she said as the doctor took supplies from a cabinet. "I know you have more important cases and all, but my mom wanted me to have my ears done by a doctor."

"Hmmph."

"Uh, will it hurt?"

The doctor turned and gave her a look so sour Kathy shut her eyes against it.

She'd just have to wait and see.

So many things in life were like that, Kathy thought, catching a whiff of rubbing alcohol, the cold of it tingling her right ear. Will it hurt? Even when the answer was yes, you never really understood it until you actually felt the pain for yourself.

Yes, it turned out, having your ears pierced hurt. But it was quick, just a couple of pings and done.

Kathy paid her ten dollars and walked out into the sunshine, hair thrown back to show the world her little gold trophies.

CHAPTER
31

EVERYONE REMEMBERED WHEN President Kennedy was shot back in November 1963. People could give you every detail—where they were that Friday, what they were doing.

Kathy had been dutifully copying the seventh-grade home ec teacher's list of the qualities of a good tossed salad into her notebook. She had just written "well drained" when the principal's strained voice crackled over the intercom with the awful news.

First, shock. Then, fear. Stupid as it sounded later, Kathy remembered thinking that if the Russians were ever going to attack—and people were always saying they were bound to—this would be the time. Now, while the United States was leaderless and vulnerable.

This time—five years later—it was different. Maybe because this Kennedy wasn't president—yet. Maybe because these assassinations were starting to seem, in some appalling way, almost routine. Obviously, this was the way it would always go. How could you claim to be shocked?

Robert Kennedy had been shot after his victory speech following the California primary, the radio reported, and Kathy could only drag through the year's last exams with the deepest, tiredest sense of What's the use? What's the use of anything?

The next day, they woke to the news of his death.

It was the last day of school, the last day with James.

She stood close to him in the hall and watched him sign a picture in Winnie's yearbook—not one of himself, but a shot of a peace symbol someone had chalked on the concrete patio the day of the walkout. "This is one sick country," he wrote.

When they went into sociology, Mrs. Redding was crying.

CHAPTER
32

DOWN BY THE river in their favorite, secret spot, James and Kathy had come for their last chance to be alone together, their last sweet nighttime moments before he had to go away. They had been kissing until they were both frantic with frustration.

"Please," James whispered. "We can't pass up this chance, can we?"

"James—"

"Remember, you're the one who said it. It's what we don't do that we regret."

"I didn't mean this, though."

"But it's what you said."

"Well, I wish I hadn't. I *regret* it, okay? I—"

He stopped her mouth with another kiss, kissing her the way surely no one else would ever be able to kiss her again, the way that zapped hot currents direct to the danger zone. Oh God. James and his talk of the resistance. Resistance? Ha! What did he know? Try acting as a one-girl resistance force against all the powers of love and nature that combined to make sure life would go on, babies would be born. No crowds cheering support. Just your own heart pounding with the confusion of trying to fight off the very one you loved. It *was* war.

"Couldn't we?" he murmured. "Just once?" His hands were sliding under her Mexican blouse.

"Somebody might come."

"No they won't."

"You always say that."

"And you always say somebody might and they don't."

Oh, everything was against her. The air was warm, the breeze was laced with the scent of freshly unfolded leaves, and between his arguing and his kissing and his hands going over her, she was slipping fast.

"It would just be so right," he insisted. "I mean, I'm leaving tomorrow. Who knows when we're ever going to see each other again? It's a perfect night. You look so pretty. This is just what I'd want to remember."

"James, please, we've talked about this a million times."

"And I would remember it," he said. "I'd remember it forever."

She pushed him back. "And you won't remember if we don't?"

"I didn't mean that. I meant—"

"Because I'm sure I'll remember this night either way."

"Well, of course, I will too. I just thought—this once—"

"Sure, just this one time and then, around the Fourth of July, I'll find out I'm pregnant, and you'll be on the other side of the country. It'll be like all those folk songs, with me wailing about my apron riding up high."

"Kathy! You think I'd be saying this if I was going to take a chance on getting you pregnant? Don't you know me better than that? Don't you trust me?" From his back pocket he pulled out a small foil square.

Her breath caught. He'd managed to buy a condom? James, who'd always been too shy even to risk being seen carrying a blanket when he walked into the woods with her?

"So?" he said.

"Uh . . ." Her mind was racing. "In health Mrs. Garvin said they could break."

"She just says that to scare people. They're probably like ninety-nine percent or something."

She hesitated. "So I could get one percent pregnant?"

"*Kathy.*"

"Well."

He made a disgusted noise. "You know, I couldn't stand to live like that—never taking the slightest risk about anything."

"But this isn't you taking the risk, is it? It's me! If we're unlucky, who's pregnant? Not you. You're gone."

"Oh, fine." He sat up, tossing the condom aside. "So I get no credit for trying to be responsible. I did that whole stupid drugstore scene for nothing."

"Oh, James," she said. "I'm sorry."

He rested his elbows on his knees, dropped his head.

"The thing is," she said, "if we were married—"

"Married!"

"I just mean if two people are married and they accidentally get pregnant, it's not such a great big horrible thing like it is if they're not."

He stood up. "Come on, let's go."

"Why?"

"Well, what's the point of staying?"

"Oh, like if you don't get your way, you don't even want to be with me?"

He shook his head. "You don't have any idea how hard this is on a guy, do you?"

Like it wasn't hard on her? She stood, brushing off bits of moss and twigs. How could he accuse her of never taking risks? He made her feel she was risking everything, holding out on him. Like he wouldn't love her unless she gave in.

On the other hand—say she did give in. What would that guarantee?

Nothing.

So tough, she thought, starting up the path. Be annoyed.

"If you knew it was gonna end up like this," he called after her, following, "you shouldn't've . . . shouldn't've . . ."

"Shouldn't've what?" She turned to face him. "Talked to you at the cast party? Kissed you in the daffodils? All the things I've been thinking *you* shouldn't've done if you'd had the slightest hint you'd be leaving?"

He flinched, surprised. She started walking again.

In the car, he started the ignition, then turned it off. "Just tell me one thing," he said, "how'd we get in so deep?"

"I don't know." She rested her elbow on the open window. "Day by day? Kiss by kiss? I mean, if there was some other place I was supposed to draw the line, I guess I missed it. And now look at us—you're leaving, and we sit here spending our last evening fighting."

"Oh, don't start that again."

"What?"

"This business where you stand back and watch us. Sometimes it's like having another person in the car."

"So sorry."

They were silent during the drive back to her house. The warm wind blew her hair around her face. What a beautiful night, she thought, to feel so perfectly miserable.

James pulled into her driveway and again they sat, Kathy wishing he would say something to make it all seem right again. Was he wishing the same?

"I know I made one mistake," she finally offered. "I see now I shouldn't have kept talking about how awful it would be to get pregnant, like that was the only thing stopping me."

"Well, isn't it? You're still freaking out over a one-in-a-hundred chance or whatever."

"Yes, but—See, you coming up with that . . . whatever you call it made me realize—even if it was guaranteed foolproof, I'd still want to wait."

"Why? I mean, if you didn't have to worry about getting pregnant—"

"Well, James, because I don't want to end up sleeping with everybody in the world, that's why."

"What are you talking about? We're just talking about you and me."

"Yeah," she said, "but the next guy'll probably say the same thing." She studied his profile in the light from the porch lamp. "I want it to be the person I marry, James, or at least the person I'm pretty sure I'll marry."

"Huh." He was still staring straight ahead. "Well, you'd know I was lying if I tried to tell you I was anywhere near ready for that."

"Fine," she said. "I know we're too young. But I'm not going to pretend I think marriage is dumb just because I'm afraid of sounding old-fashioned."

"I never said—"

"Because actually, I can't think of anything better. I want somebody to hang on to. And he hangs on to me. And we have each other to go through whatever life throws at us. I want that, okay? I admit it."

They fell silent again for a while; then James heaved a big sigh.

"I've only got one thing to say in my defense—"

"You don't have to defend yourself—"

"Just listen, okay? I've always had this idea your first ought to be somebody you really loved."

She waited.

"And I love you, okay?"

She nodded.

"Even if I'm acting mad."

"I know," she said. "I love you too."

"So I just wanted you to be my first, that's all."

"Oh, James." Words. Lovely words. For her, the hardest thing to resist. She pulled his hand off the steering wheel and held it. "First would be nice," she said, "but . . ."

"What," he said flatly.

"Well, I'm holding out for more. I want to be somebody's last."

"Last?"

She nodded. "Last." She made him look right into her eyes. "As in, ever after."

CHAPTER
33

ON THE SOUTH side of the gray stone train station, Kathy and James sat close together on an old wooden baggage wagon, watching the curved approach of the tracks to the south.

"Shouldn't it be here by now?" James said.

Kathy pulled her watch from her jeans pocket. "Yeah, it's late. I hope you don't end up missing your connection East."

He shrugged. "I could always sleep in the station or something."

A pang shot to her heart at this image—James wandering alone through the Portland station.

"Do your parents know when you're coming into Boston?"

"Sort of. But I told them I'll phone. They say the trains are late a lot."

She nodded, sighing. Funny, she'd always imagined a train station farewell would be so romantic. But maybe romantic looked better than it felt. The girl in that drawing she'd done last year might have looked moody as all get out, but she didn't have a clue about the ache Kathy had in her chest, doing this scene for real.

"Won't your parents be surprised," she said, "about you making the front page?" Last night's paper had featured a picture of Robert Kennedy on the Benton County Courthouse steps, one of his last campaign stops before leaving Oregon for California. California and death.

"You can hardly tell it's me," James said, "in the crowd."

"Yes, you can. *I* can." The caption called the group Kennedy supporters. James's McCarthy sign was turned sideways and didn't show. "Crashing the Kennedy rally. You're such a rabble-rouser."

"I try."

Kathy leaned forward on her hands and gave him a sly sideways smile. "You know who's going to miss you next year? The vice principal."

"Right."

"Really, it's going to be so boring for him, not having you to drag offstage or whatever."

"Ah, but just think of the vice principal at my new school!"

"Yeah." Kathy sat up. "I can see him now. School's out. He's celebrating, sitting there with a cold beer, no idea what's going to be heading toward him on the train."

They lapsed into silence, Kathy swinging her feet. It was nice, she thought, the way the branch of the station's lone maple arched over the view of the place where the train was due to appear.

"It shouldn't be sunny," she said after a while.

"Huh?"

186

"It should be gray. Sad scenes shouldn't look too cheerful."

"Oh. Right." He hopped off the cart. "I'm going to see if they know what's going on."

Kathy picked at a flake of the baggage cart's peeling blue paint. Did he have to act so anxious? And yet somehow she wanted this over with too.

"Anytime," he said, coming back.

She slid down and leaned against him. "Did I tell you Helen Keller died Saturday? I felt bad because . . . actually I hadn't thought about her still being alive. I could have written her. Told her how much I admired her and all that. And now it's too late."

"Hmm. A genuine regret."

"Guess so." She gave him a rueful smile. "Don't worry, James. We have our whole lives ahead of us to be regretful. You'll find plenty of stuff to write about."

They watched a boy run out and lay pennies on the track for the train wheels to flatten.

"You'll write me, won't you?" she asked.

"Hey, I've only promised a hundred times."

"And phone?" The sound of his voice was something she was going to miss desperately. "I know it costs a fortune, though."

"I can do it once in a while."

"And why did stamps have to go up just when you're leaving? Six cents!"

"I think we can afford that."

"I know," she said, "but my letters are going to be thick. I doubt one stamp will do it."

"Kathy, when are you going to admit it? *You're* the writer."

"Maybe we'll *both* be writers."

"Hey, yeah. And this'll be one of those famous literary correspondences. They'll publish them all in a book someday."

She winced. "I hope not. I mean, I hope you won't write like you're figuring that's what'll happen. You know, planning out what you say instead of just sort of talking on paper."

"Don't worry."

"You know, James, sometimes people swear they'll write and phone and nothing can break them up and then they meet other people and they forget."

"Yeah." He stared off down the tracks. "And sometimes people write and phone and get back together the very first chance."

She looked at him. "You think it'll be that way? For us?"

"Maybe. It could." He ran his hand through her hair. "Meet you at Stanford, right? Or Berkeley?"

"You know my folks don't want me to go down there."

"You can convince them."

She sighed, weary at the thought of the arguments ahead. "But what about New York? What if I decide to skip college and go straight to Broadway and try to break in as an actress?"

He smiled. "That's even better. It'll be no trick at all to find you if your name's up in lights."

"Oh, James."

How strange, trying to imagine the future. Not just next week, next year—but the future as in *I wonder how our lives will turn out.*

She was terrible at imagining herself older. For one thing, she always saw herself taller—a screwy idea, obviously, since she hadn't grown a fraction of an inch since seventh grade and wasn't likely to start up again now. But still, she would definitely be more sophisticated. When she was much older, in her twenties, she'd wear black, she figured. She would not talk so much or walk so fast. She'd be mysterious. People would wonder about her . . .

She'd turn into a different person? Ha!

And James? She tried to picture him as a real writer. Maybe he'd wear one of those tweed jackets with leather patches on the elbows. And smoke a pipe?

And how would he write *her* if she was a character in one of his books? It'd be nice if he'd make her a little prettier than she really was, and cut out a few of the dumber things she'd said.

And then she had an unsettling thought. "James? Do you think you'll ever write about . . . you know, down by the river, when we . . ."

"Uh . . ." His face flushed. "I don't know. Writers are supposed to be able to write about anything, I guess, but that would be . . ."

She nodded, relieved. She didn't necessarily want to see *everything* in print. But a book about the two of them would be nice, and what a sad, beautiful story it would be. They'd probably make it into a movie. And she'd be sitting in the balcony down at the Whiteside, watching it, knowing the girl saying goodbye forever in the train station scene was her, but not telling a soul, just weeping and weeping. "What's the matter, honey?" her husband would say. This imaginary husband had an oddly blank face, of course, seeing as how she couldn't imagine ever loving or marrying anyone but James . . .

"So what are you going to do the rest of the summer?" James said.

"Hmm? Oh, cry a lot. Write to you."

"You better get out and do more than that or you'll hear from me about it."

"Yeah, yeah. Well, I might try out for one of the Barn Theater plays, or offer to paint sets or something. Look for a job. What about you?"

"Probably see if there's anything I can do on the McCarthy campaign back there."

She nodded, already picturing him down at headquarters, hustling around with the Clean for Gene volunteer girls. Probably the very first one he met would be big on free love. Maybe she'd be older, already in college, with her own funky little apartment where she'd take him. On the wall above her bed she'd have that draft resistance poster with Joan Baez and Mimi Farina—"Girls Say Yes to Boys Who Say No."

Oh, stop it! Making up stories like this could drive her nuts in no time.

"I doubt McCarthy's got much of a chance," James went on, "but my dad heard they might send some busloads of kids to the convention."

"In Chicago?"

"Yeah, and somehow I have this feeling I want to be there."

"You know, James, sometimes I don't think you're going to be a writer at all. You'll be a professional . . . what's that word? Agitator!"

"Maybe so. I guess I'm actually better at flinging words around for people to hear than I am at nailing them down to paper. Besides, one crazed writer in a relationship is probably enough."

"You mean me?"

"Uh . . ." He looked around theatrically. "Is there

anyone else in this relationship you haven't told me about?"

She smiled. "Oh, James. You realize you make me laugh better than anyone else in the world? And now what am I going to do? I'll probably just be sad for the rest of my life."

"No, you won't."

"Promise?"

He nodded, drawing her close. "Hey, I'm really sorry about . . . you know . . . hassling you last night." He tucked the wild rose dangling against her cheek back into her hair. "Sometimes I get kind of crazy."

She looked off past him. "It's okay." But would it be? Would she regret holding out on him? Passing up what might have been the last chance in their whole lives? She sighed. The answer to this one would probably be years in coming.

And now they heard the whistle. The train's headlight appeared around the curve and slowly, ominously moved toward them. Then the roar of the machine itself engulfed them and the train braked to a shrill stop.

A handful of passengers got off two cars down. A half dozen more hustled from the station and clustered at the open door to board.

James pulled his backpack from the cart and flung it over his shoulder. "I guess this is it."

Oh, no. Wait. Suddenly, after all this horrible dragging out, it was going to be over too fast. She pressed her face against his chest and inhaled. How long would it be before she felt these arms around her again? Would she ever? She lifted her face and they kissed.

"Ooops, I almost forgot." He dug in his jeans

pocket, then opened his fist. On his palm lay two charms. "Which half do you want?"

The silver bits winked at her through sudden tears. "A cracked heart," she said wonderingly. "You remembered."

He glanced over his shoulder. Everyone else had boarded. "Hey, hurry, okay?"

"Oh, James." She sniffed, blinking desperately. "What do they say? I can't even focus."

"True. And love."

"Oh, perfect."

"All aboard!"

She took one without looking and flung an arm around him, hurrying with him toward the train.

He stopped and held her. His breath warm in her ear, he whispered, "I'll be back." Then, gently unfastening himself from her embrace, he ran the rest of the way to the train and jumped on.

Without noise or fanfare the train began to slide forward. One last wave, she thought, but she couldn't find him in any of the windows. She started to hurry alongside. No use. She stopped.

So. Farewell.

She stood there as the cars clicked past, gathering speed.

In no time the train had curved out of sight beneath the highway overpass, its whistle sounding at the next crossing ahead.

The boy scampered out to collect his pennies, giving a little whoop as he spotted each one.

In two minutes, the station was empty. Kathy stood there with the oddest, emptiest feeling. Now what?

One of the baggage handlers gave her a curious look.

Then she remembered, and opened her tightly clenched fist.

True.

She wondered if she might cry, but somehow she didn't feel like it. Was that because she'd been crying her eyes out for three weeks? Or because she wasn't really lonely yet? Or—

My God, she thought, her mother was right—this self-consciousness just couldn't be normal!

She slipped the cracked heart into her pocket and headed back to the car. Easing into the driver's seat, she gazed dully through the windshield at the freight cars parked across the tracks.

Amazing, to think of everything that had happened since James's life had intersected with hers. Too bad she hadn't kept a diary. After all, no matter what happened next, this *had* turned out to be the story of the first true love of her life.

Was it too late to write it all down now? She still remembered every detail, and it was obviously the only thing she'd be thinking about for a long time to come. And what if James didn't become a writer and make a novel out of this? *Somebody* ought to.

She couldn't write only about him, though. To understand why he'd meant so much, how he'd lit up her life, she'd have to tell about Gary, and how bewildered she'd been over exactly who to be. She'd have to write about the way life, before, had somehow looked so dark.

And if she changed things a little just to make a better story, it would still have to be true. True, like on her silver heart. A true that ran deeper than literal, it-happened-exactly-this-way true.

And it would be long. Pages and pages. Writer's cramp, for sure.

Unless . . .

Oh, brother. The joke was on her.

She was going to have to break down and get out that typewriter.

EPILOGUE

KATHY AND JAMES wrote letters until they each had a couple of shoe boxes full, but eventually, as the stream of mail slowed to a trickle, Kathy lost heart for shutting out the new guys who came around. What was she supposed to say? Sorry, I'm busy writing a love letter to a guy who hardly ever writes back anymore?

One thing led to another—likewise with James—and by the time they were college seniors, they were both talking marriage, and not to each other.

But when James's bride-to-be suggested meeting him at the altar to the guitar-strummed strains of "Scarborough Fair," an alarm went off in his heart.

Jumping into his wooden-bumpered VW van one spring weekend, he drove nonstop from Berkeley to Lewis and Clark College in Portland, walked into Kathy's dorm, and called her from the lobby.

"It's James!" she told her fiancé as she dashed back into her room from the hall phone.

"Not the guy," he said, rising from her desk chair, "where you wrote that . . . story."

195

"That's right. Him!" She whirled to the mirror, madly flailing her hairbrush. They'd been having one of their boring-beyond-belief arguments; she couldn't have invented a more thrilling interruption. "He's downstairs, right this minute!"

"Now, don't be too quick to—"

She flew down the stairs to the lounge, catching herself on the doorjamb at the bottom, breathless.

James stood up from the sofa and turned around.

James. She couldn't believe it—to see him, not in her imagination as she had so many times over these years, but truly standing there, living and breathing.

"I thought I should come find you," he said, "before I . . ."

From that moment, both their engagements were doomed.

After a month of desperate long-distance calls and insane up-and-down-the-freeway drives, Kathy and James agreed that in the interest of avoiding two potential cases of dead serious, lifelong regret, they had no business thinking of marrying anyone but each other.

SO.

Happily ever after?

Sure, why not? Or as close as true love comes in the real world.

Twenty-four years later they live near San Francisco, where James is a lawyer for the American Civil Liberties Union, specializing in police practices, an interest dating to the 1968 Democratic Convention and the beating he received at the hands of Chicago's finest.

Kathy never could stop herself from trying to turn real life into stories. Now she writes novels that are published in New York, a city where, to this day, she has yet to set foot.

Best of all, in the 1980s minivans were invented, meaning neither of them ever had to suffer the indignity of driving their daughters to soccer practice in a station wagon.

ABOUT THE AUTHOR

LINDA CREW was born and brought up in Corvallis, Oregon, where she now lives on Wake Robin Farm with her husband, Herb, and their children, Miles, Mary, and William. Her other books are *Nekomah Creek,* an ALA Notable Book; *Nekomah Creek Christmas; Someday I'll Laugh About This; Fire on the Wind;* and *Children of the River,* which won the International Reading Association Children's Book Award for 1990 in the Older Reader Category, was chosen as a Best Book for Young Adults by the American Library Association, and was the 1989 Honor Book for the Golden Kite Award, given by the Society of Children's Book Writers.